About th

Scott Hunter was born in Romford, Essex in 1956. He was educated at Douai School in Woolhampton, Berkshire. His writing career began after he won first prize in the Sunday Express short story competition in 1996. He currently combines writing with a parallel career as a semi-professional drummer. He lives in Berkshire with his wife and a modest collection of drums.

THE FRAGILE COAST

Scott Hunter

A Myrtle Villa Book

Originally published in Great Britain by Myrtle Villa
Publishing

Acknowledgements

Thanks as always to my insightful and excellent editor, Louise Maskill, and a very special thank you to Gladis for correcting my erroneous Spanish translations. Any remaining errors are down to me…

For Mr Davies, who taught me how to spell
necessary

'A trustworthy spy is a dangerous ally…'
—Unknown

Author's Note

On January 17, 1966, at the height of the Cold War, a United States bomber and a tanker collided above the small farming village of Palomares, Spain, during a routine midair refuelling operation. The explosion killed seven airmen and scattered the bomber's payload—four unarmed thermonuclear bombs—across miles of coastline.

One bomb fell into the Mediterranean where the US Navy, with great difficulty, salvaged it two and a half months later. The remaining three fell inland; two burst open and dispersed plutonium with the wind. The contaminated land was partially cleaned, and the United States shipped radioactive dirt and debris to America for disposal.

So, four bombs.

Or was it five?

Easy to lose count of a bomber's payload … especially if you can't find it all.

What could possibly go wrong?

SH, May 2025

1

12th September, 1971.

Kyle had been watching the passenger in the second row since they'd boarded the ramshackle coach outside his hotel in central Cairo. The rest of the passengers were unmistakably tourists, as he was himself; not so the occupant of the window seat two rows behind the driver.

Kyle disliked pigeon-holing himself as a tourist, but recognised that there was no escaping the fact. He was here to escape London's grey ceiling and to try to forget that he was a dead man walking – not the easiest thing to relegate to the back of one's mind at the best of times, but he'd reasoned that foreign travel might, at the very least, ease his mental burden and help him make the most of the time he had left – in the words of his neurosurgeon an unguessable statistic he'd be well advised not to dwell upon.

The destination had proved a harder choice than he'd anticipated, but after several visits to his local travel agent he'd eventually decided on Egypt, a country now deemed safe to visit following the cessation of Egyptian/Israeli hostilities a year earlier. As a child he'd always been fascinated by the Pyramids, the Sphinx, the legends of the Nile, the Valley of the Kings; the names alone evoked mystery, history, the colours and scents of an older world. Kyle wanted to see it all.

Which was why he now found himself rattling along poorly-maintained roads in a coach that looked and felt as though it had been rescued from the scrapyard and given a fresh coat of paint to cover the worst signs of wear and tear. The driver was a small, dark man who appeared to have little regard for the comfort of his passengers, or anyone else careless enough to get in his way. The horn blared almost continually, and pedestrians and cars scattered at their approach.

The tour guide, a slim elegant young woman in a red blouse and denim flares, seemed unfazed by their lurching progress. Kyle glanced at her as she balanced herself between two seats with an expertise born of long practice and raised her microphone to her lips.

'Good morning, ladies and gentlemen. Thank you for joining our tour to Giza…'

Her accent was discernible, but her English was perfect, her pronunciation accurate, and her words as clear as a bell as they popped through the tinny speakers above the racket of the coach's labouring engine. However, Kyle wasn't listening; his attention remained focused on the man in the second row. The man who looked all wrong.

Kyle's fellow passengers were a mixture of Britons, Europeans and Americans; most were middle-aged, although a few, like the couple immediately in front of Kyle, were closer to his age or perhaps slightly older. Kyle's object of interest was different. He looked to be of Arab or Israeli origin, Turkish maybe? Hard to say. He was bearded, clad in scruffy jeans and a sweat-stained, open-necked shirt, and wore his fashionably long hair gathered into a loose ponytail.

His head was never still, turning this way and that as they made slow progress out of the city. The seat beside him was empty, as though the other passengers had instinctively given him a wide berth, perhaps assuming him to be a friend or relative of the driver, or perhaps the tour guide's minder, or relative.

It was a long time since Kyle had served as a detective constable in the Met, but he could still recognise a villain when he saw one. This guy had villain written all over him.

The tour guide was coming to the end of her spiel. '… we will reach our destination in approximately twenty minutes. Until then, make yourselves comfortable and enjoy the trip.'

Kyle admired the tour guide's shapely curves as she took her seat. The man with the beard paid her no attention, instead continuing to scan the road on either side and ahead. He reminded Kyle of a fighter pilot checking the skies for enemy aircraft.

A robbery? Tourists were always fair game for a quick fleecing, but that usually happened on the streets and in the souks; much less likely here, enclosed in this tin coffin with just a few travellers' cheques as reward. No, not a robbery; Kyle was forming a distinct impression leaning more towards violence than thievery. He wasn't an avid follower of the news, but it had been impossible to avoid the press coverage of the still-simmering hostilities between Egypt and Israel. Sure, a ceasefire had been agreed, but the situation nevertheless remained highly volatile. The powers-that-be might have decreed that North Africa was now a safe-to-travel zone, but the reality was that anything could kick off at any time.

Not that it bothered Kyle. He was on death row anyway.

The coach slowed and the driver leaned on his horn, this time more persistently. Kyle stood up for a better look. They had cleared the built up area and traffic was now sparse. The glare of the sun made him squint but through the front windscreen he could see that a vehicle, an open-topped truck, was parked across the road a few hundred metres ahead, effectively blocking their way. The coach driver muttered something unintelligible in Arabic and made an exasperated gesture, the meaning of which wasn't hard to interpret.

The tour guide stood up for a better look, holding on firmly to the seat headrest in front of her as the coach moved forward again, this time at a more cautious pace. Kyle made his way along the aisle to the front.

'Problem?'

The tour guide turned her head towards him and did her best to offer a reassuring smile, but Kyle wasn't fooled. The driver was still crawling forward in second gear, cursing under his breath.

'Tell him to stop the coach,' Kyle said.

The tour guide was wearing a name badge, *Nadira*. She frowned, a slight creasing of her forehead. 'I'm sure everything is OK, sir. If you could please return to your…'

'You don't believe that,' Kyle interrupted. 'I'm sure you don't want to take any chances with your passengers' safety.' He pointed at the truck. 'Look, they're not broken down. If they were, they'd be parked at the roadside, not across it.'

Nadira pursed her lips as she considered Kyle's observation. Behind them, the passengers seated towards the front of the coach had begun to cotton on that there was some kind of issue. A low muttering began, an exchange of half-formed queries and anxious whispers.

Kyle was positioned parallel to the man with the ponytail. No more head movements; now Kyle's attention was entirely focused on the guy's hands, one levering himself upright using the front seat headrest, and the other snaking into his pocket.

Kyle didn't wait to see what he was trying to retrieve. He

scythed his arm a hundred and eighty degrees to the left and felt a crunch of cartilage as the edge of his hand smashed into ponytail's windpipe. He followed through with a fist to the man's head, slamming his skull against the window. Kyle bent and retrieved the automatic that had slipped from the guy's pocket onto the sun-faded seat cover beside him.

'*Now* stop the coach,' Kyle ordered, pointing the automatic directly at the driver's head. No time for persuasion or reasoning – not that Kyle spoke the language anyway – and certainly not now that three armed men had appeared from behind the blockade and were walking purposefully towards them. The driver got the idea and brought them quickly to a standstill. Nadira's hands were shaking as she picked up the microphone, but her voice was steady. 'Please remain in your seats for the moment. Thank you ladies and gentlemen.'

Kyle was impressed with her coolness, but the passengers deserved a little more. 'Tell them to keep their heads down – please.'

She nodded and issued the additional instruction in a calm, reassuring tone and the fretful murmurs were instantly superseded by a compliant, albeit tense, silence.

Kyle was impressed all over again; Nadira would handle the passengers. His job was to stay focused on the three approaching guys in headscarves and camo jackets. Not army, not police. Some splinter faction, maybe, with a grudge against the UK or US? Right now the whys and wherefores didn't matter. Best to concentrate on the three men as they drew closer, confidently assuming, so Kyle hoped, that their onboard accomplice had taken control of the coach as planned. Surprise was always a great advantage when the odds were stacked against you, and right now it was the only advantage he was likely to get.

Question was, what was their objective? A hijack and subsequent ransom demand? Or just a full-scale massacre?

Kyle scrutinised the trio as two of them fell slightly behind the one on the left The leader. That was good to know.

'Does the door open automatically?' Kyle asked without taking his eyes from the threat.

'Yes,' Nadira said. 'To Omar's right, by the gear shift.' She nodded towards the driver.

'Tell him to open it.'

Nadira frowned. 'We can't just let them in. They'll...'

Kyle silenced her with a look. He hoped it wasn't too fierce; more of a *trust me* kind of expression. Either way, it had the desired effect. Nadira issued a terse command to Omar who leaned forward without question and pulled the lever. The door creaked open on protesting hydraulics.

Kyle stepped forward and found the gap between the coach body and the open door, nestled the automatic in the small space and shot the leader in the head. The guy went down hard, slamming into the dirt. His two companions froze, and then acted as Kyle had anticipated; one darted around the front of the coach to his right while the other broke into a crouching run, heading left. Kyle now had to figure out who would shoot first. The one on the left seemed a likelier candidate – he'd already unslung his automatic rifle.

Kyle dragged the body of the ponytailed accomplice from the seat, dumped him on the floor, smashed the window with the butt of the automatic and took a potshot at the running man. He missed, but the guy stopped running, squatted and raised his rifle. Bullets sprayed along the coach body, tracking towards Kyle. He ducked as the nearest window exploded in a shower of glass. A woman screamed.

Kyle lifted his head a fraction, snapped off a second shot. The man was running again and so was a moving target, but luck was with Kyle and the bullet found a mark just below the guy's knee. He howled and collapsed onto the scrubby earth, both hands clutching his wound. He then seemed to recognize his predicament and made a grab for his weapon, rolling onto his back and lifting the barrel towards the coach. Kyle shot him in the chest. He fell back and lay still.

Kyle paused. One assailant left, position unknown. If roles were reversed, what would he do? A coach full of people, one defender with a pistol. First, stay close, use the cover. Second, think smart. The windows were too high to simply poke a rifle through and open fire. They'd been expecting to simply climb on board, no resistance, but things hadn't gone to plan.

So … if the guy had any sense, he'd try to manufacture his own element of surprise. Would he sidle up against the body of the coach? Not on Kyle's side, because he'd know that Kyle could simply dip out the door and shoot him. On the other side, however, away from the door, he could creep along below the level of the windows, nip around to the front and open fire through the windscreen before anyone had time to react. Risky, but a possibility.

There were two further options, though: the roof, and underneath. Kyle rejected the former. No way could the guy get on the roof without being seen, and it wouldn't offer much of an advantage anyway. No; if he was really smart he'd go for the latter. He'd crawl under the coach until he was just beneath the door, wait for Kyle to show himself, and then it'd be game over.

Unless Kyle took the initiative. No more time to waste. Apart from his wits and the automatic, what else did he have at his disposal? The coach's engine was still running, Omar's hands still on the steering wheel – maybe through force of habit or just for want of somewhere better to put them. Kyle made a decision. 'Nadira, tell the driver to reverse hard, fast as he can.'

She nodded, spoke rapidly to Omar.

The engine roared and the coach jerked into reverse. A heartbeat later it lurched over an unseen obstruction, canting violently to the left to a chorus of terrified screams from the passengers. The vehicle teetered momentarily on two wheels before righting itself and slamming back to earth with an impact that made Kyle's teeth rattle.

Omar kept going; someone towards the back began to shout the opening words of the Lord's Prayer. As they continued to weave drunkenly backwards, Kyle reached over and placed a restraining hand on the driver's shoulder. 'OK, Omar. You can stop now.'

The coach skidded to a halt in a flurry of dust.

Kyle squinted through the haze. A bundle of bloody rags lay by the roadside.

The third man.

'Better relay the good news,' Kyle said to Nadira. He was overcome by a sudden light-headedness; he dropped into the nearest seat and put his head between his legs. Either the heat had finally got to him, or the adrenaline. Maybe a bit of both.

Nadira made her announcement. Somewhere in the distance, police sirens struck up a discordant harmony. The sound of approaching officialdom broke the tension; the driver lit a cigarette and conversation began to bubble excitedly along the coach's length. A woman across the aisle dabbed a handkerchief to her husband's forehead with a shaky hand; a splinter of glass had incised a small wound, but aside from that there didn't appear to be any other casualties.

Nadira sat down next to him. 'Thank you. That was ... I don't know what to say. How did you know what to do?'

Kyle lifted his head a fraction. It felt thick and muzzy, but he managed a thin smile. 'A long time ago...' He hesitated and took a breath. It felt as though what he was about to say was nothing to do with him, that he was ascribing some random person's former identity to himself.

'A *very* long time ago,' he said, 'I used to be a policeman.'

2

'I never got to see them,' Kyle replied, lighting a cigarette. He dropped the match into the glass ashtray beside his armchair and exhaled a thin stream of smoke.

His visitor coughed politely and raised an eyebrow. 'I didn't have you down as a smoker.'

'No?' Kyle shrugged. 'Thought I'd take it up, just for the hell of it. Passes the time.' He shot the man a wry smile. 'You'd better update your most secret file.'

'I'll make a point of it,' the man replied. 'But let's get back to Giza. You say that you flew home twenty-four hours after the incident? You didn't want to take another tour to see the Sphinx, the Pyramids?'

'Would you, under the circumstances?' Kyle shrugged. 'As I said, I never got to see them. Sightseeing wasn't foremost in my mind when I got back to the hotel. If the Cairo police hadn't held me up I'd have been on a plane the same evening.'

'Of course. I understand.' The man crossed one leg over the other. He seemed at ease, relaxed. His suit was elegantly cut, Savile Row by the look of it, and pricey. His hair was Brylcreemed across his forehead in a sleek U-shape, an attempt to disguise the fact that he was prematurely receding.

Kyle put him in his mid-thirties. Senior. Successful. He wondered when this smooth official would get to the point.

The few days since Kyle's return from Egypt had been uneventful. His return flight to Heathrow had passed without incident, the cool, smoggy air that greeted him as he crossed the tarmac to the arrivals building a welcome tonic after Cairo's oppressive heat. He found his apartment just as he had left it; an abandoned, half-drunk mug of tea still sitting on his kitchen table, the remnants of his hurried breakfast stacked accusingly in the enamel sink. But then, although it felt as though he'd been away for weeks, he'd only been gone forty-eight hours. What had he expected?

That night, the dreams had begun. The coach, the blazing sun; masked men leering through the shattered windows, the passengers all dead except himself and the driver. Delayed shock, of course. He'd acted out of pure instinct at the time, but he knew he'd been lucky. It was a long time since he'd held a firearm, but his marksmanship had been accurate enough on the day.

Lucky? Maybe. The oddest thing was that the whole episode had awakened something inside himself he'd thought long dead; he'd realised that he wanted to go on living. This was an unexpected turnaround after the bleak, nihilistic months that had preceded his ill-fated trip, and Kyle was trying his damnedest to come to terms with it. Nothing had changed, medically speaking. The bullet fragment was still lodged deep in his brain, ready to kill him at a moment's notice, but now, instead of embracing the possibility of sudden extinction, he found himself railing against it.

'I expect you're wondering why a civil service official has called to see you,' the man interrupted his reverie.

'Not to discuss my police pension, I shouldn't imagine.'

The man issued a short, dry laugh. 'Indeed not.' He slipped his hand deftly into his jacket pocket and withdrew a business card. He stretched across the short space between them.

Kyle stuck his cigarette in his mouth, took the proffered card with a muttered thanks and read aloud, 'Jacob Stanhope. Century House, Westminster Bridge Road, Lambeth, London.' He placed the card on the occasional table next to his ashtray. 'Ah. I wasn't far off the mark. Not the Department of Health, I take it?'

'No.'

'Thought not,' Kyle said. 'The NHS have pretty much written me off.'

Stanhope hesitated. 'Your ... condition is relevant to my reason for being here, but not in a curative sense, I'm afraid.'

'I see.' Kyle took a final drag of the cigarette and stubbed its remains out in the ashtray. 'And here was I hoping for a miracle.'

'Sorry to disappoint.' Stanhope's mouth formed an awkward smile. 'Your health – and possible medical interventions – are not the purpose of my visit. I'm more interested in the psychology of your condition, as are my superiors – and even more so following your recent notable performance in Cairo.'

'Let's cut to the chase,' Kyle said. 'Security services, correct?'

'I've given you my card,' Stanhope said. 'I'm not hiding the fact.'

Kyle recognised that, in Stanhope's world, nothing would be explicitly revealed, only implied.

'Allow me to elaborate,' Stanhope went on. 'You're an ex-policeman. You have a life-threatening injury, but despite that, a short while ago you were instrumental in ridding us of a minor irritant in the shape of a certain gentleman from Italy, a small-time extortionist with plans to escalate his activity into areas that would have caused us – how can I put this? –

ah, certain inconveniences.'

Kyle was shocked. 'You know about that? But how—'

'We know because we know. It's what we do.' Stanhope brushed an imaginary mote of dust from his meticulously creased trousers. 'And then, lo and behold, you resurface in Cairo, an ordinary tourist by all accounts, but somehow you manage to single-handedly take out a group of disgruntled Israeli dissidents, thus saving a coach load of innocents from a most unpleasant fate.'

'It was a knee-jerk reaction. Anyone could have done the same.'

'I think not, Mr Kyle. And neither do my superiors.'

'I just want to forget it,' Kyle said. 'It happened. It's over. I don't see the relevance.' Kyle's felt his heart rate slowing to something close to its normal rhythm. Stanhope's reference to the Welsh incident had been unexpected and unsettling. What else did this dapper, urbane man know about him?

Stanhope nodded, pursed his lips. 'Understandable. But as I say, my superiors have formed an opinion concerning your good self, and would like to make you a proposition.'

That sounded ominous. 'Go on.' Kyle toyed with the lid of his cigarette pack. 'Let's hear it.'

Stanhope looked pleased. 'Good. Mr Kyle, you may or may not not be aware of a rather embarrassing incident that occurred over Spanish airspace a few years ago. It wasn't covered up, per se, but at the request of our friends across the pond neither was it over-reported, if you get my drift.' Stanhope made quotation marks in the air to illustrate his point. 'The location was Almeria – Palomares to be specific – just off the south coast of Spain. A USAF B52 was refuelling at 31,000 feet, but unfortunately collided with its refuelling Stratotanker.'

'I vaguely recall, but I don't see—'

Stanhope raised his hand. 'Bear with me. All will become

clear.' He smiled, a fleeting, quizzical expression.

Kyle shrugged. He had nothing else planned for the day.

'Seven crew members were killed. Tragic, of course, but the nub of the problem was the payload. According to US intelligence, the B52 was carrying four thermonuclear hydrogen bombs. Three hit the ground, one fell into the sea. The non-nuclear explosive elements in two of the bombs exploded on impact, contaminating two square kilometres of Almerian soil with radioactive plutonium.'

'Good grief.'

'Quite so.'

'And the fourth?'

'Fell into the sea. It was undamaged, and quickly recovered. Fortunately for the Americans, a local fisherman witnessed its trajectory and was able to identify its rough location on the sea bed.'

'So what's the issue? I suppose there must have been some kind of cleanup of the affected area inland?'

'There was, but according to the Spanish, it wasn't thorough enough. There's still a great deal of wrangling going on between Spain and the US regarding the efficacy of the decontamination. The local farmers are understandably unhappy that a sizeable chunk of their land has been sealed off, and the local residents are concerned, also understandably, about the risks to the health of their families.'

Kyle nodded. 'All right. But the threat's been more or less contained. So…?'

'Indeed – or so we also fondly imagined. However, it has recently come to our attention that we were … spun a line, I think is the American expression.'

'How so?' Despite himself, Kyle was intrigued. He lit a second cigarette and extinguished the match with a flick of his thumbnail.

Stanhope cleared his throat. 'Apparently there was a fifth

bomb, which also fell into the sea. A different animal altogether. They tried to locate it, but drew a blank. So they hushed it up, big time.' The American slang sounded strange in Stanhope's clipped public school English accent.

'How different?'

Stanhope moistened his lips. 'It was biological. Potent.'

'Bioweapons? Good God.'

'Anthrax, to be precise, in this particular case,.'

Kyle took a deep drag of his cigarette. 'Nasty. But I thought Nixon put the kibosh on the US bioweapons programme last year?'

Stanhope nodded. 'He did indeed, and the majority of their arsenal has, by now, been destroyed. Which is why this whole issue has become such an embarrassment.'

'But why can't the Yanks just collect the bomb and dispose of it?'

'Ah, therein lies the problem,' Stanhope said, uncrossing his leg and smoothing his trousers with what seemed to be an habitual gesture. 'Unfortunately, it wasn't the Americans who eventually located the missing item.'

'Don't tell me.' Kyle guessed what was coming.

Stanhope compressed his lips. 'You've guessed it. Brezhnev and his crew somehow got wind of it, and we've become aware of Russian activity in the area.'

'And if they do recover the bomb, what's to stop them setting it off and pointing the finger elsewhere?

'Precisely,' Stanhope said. 'The original plutonium problem will seem like a walk in the park for those poor Spanish peasants.'

'OK, so now the obvious question.' Kyle cocked his head.

'What has all this got to do with an ex-detective constable?'

'I can see why you were an obvious candidate for the SIS recruitment team.' Kyle closed his eyes for a moment as his headache moved up a notch on what he referred to as the

Kyle scale. It had been hovering at around four and a half when Stanhope knocked on his door. Now, as was usually the case when he was engaged in an extended conversation, it was on the move in the wrong direction. If it got to a six he'd customarily resort to codeine. Any higher meant the bedroom and drawn curtains until it subsided.

'Still troubling you, the headaches?' For a split second, a look of what seemed to be genuine concern creased Stanhope's forehead.

'You know about those, of course.' Kyle narrowed his eyes. 'Along with my inside leg measurement, my—'

'Yes, we know a great deal about you, Mr Kyle. And, to answer your question as succinctly as possible, I – or, I should say, *we* – would like to make you an offer.'

'Namely?'

'Work for us for a short period. You'll be looked after financially, and well supported in the field.'

'Now, hold on a minute—'

Stanhope's hand was up again. 'Hear me out.'

Kyle exhaled smoke through both nostrils and nodded. 'All right.'

Stanhope went on. 'The bomb has been located, but it has not yet been salvaged. According to our contacts, though, the operation will shortly be underway; clandestine, obviously, probably in the guise of a fishing vessel. If the device is successfully salvaged, as I anticipate will be the case, then, as you say, there will be nothing to stop our chilly friends from arranging a detonation – accidental or otherwise is immaterial – which will have a devastating effect on the surrounding area. Inhalation is almost always fatal.' Stanhope paused to allow his words to sink in.

Kyle was horrified. He stubbed out his cigarette and stared hard at the carpet. The notion that anyone might consider releasing such a deadly agent in a peaceful agricultural environment was outrageous.

'Dreadful, in terms of the human cost, of course,' Stanhope continued, 'but in terms of the big picture, not the worst consequence.'

Kyle looked up. 'No?'

'No. Naturally, Russia will deny all knowledge, leaving the US to shoulder one hundred percent of the blame. Europe as a whole will side with Spain, and the US will be nothing less than a pariah. Which will suit Brezhnev very nicely.'

'Politics.' Kyle shook his head.

'The Cold War is yet to thaw to any significant degree,' Stanhope reminded him. 'It's only been nine years since Cuba.'

Kyle leaned back and regarded Stanhope through slitted eyes. 'Why me? You must have dozens of available operatives.'

'If only that were the case.' Stanhope smiled sadly. 'To tell the truth, we lost a couple recently. One in Berlin, and one in Almeria – oh, and a reporter has also disappeared in the area. We think she was getting a bit too close to the truth.'

'Even so, the answer's no,' Kyle said, levering himself out of his chair. 'I'll show you out.'

'I understand.' Stanhope rose. 'But I hope you might reconsider when I tell you the name of the reporter.'

'I doubt that.' Kyle held the sitting room door open.

'A Miss Jude Bates. You know her quite well, I believe?'

3

'Bates? But she's serving time.' Kyle released the door and it banged shut. 'She went down for two years – manslaughter.'
'She did. But she lodged an appeal twelve months in.' Stanhope faced Kyle across the hall. 'And she found help – well-qualified help, from an ex-colleague of a Mr. Sven Jörgensen. You'll remember him too, I imagine.'
Kyle said nothing.
'A good sort.' Stanhope moved seamlessly over Kyle's silence. 'Chap by the name of Peter Wiltshire. Quite the terrier in court, apparently; heading rapidly for QC even at the tender age of twenty-nine. Heard what had happened re said Swede – the parts that were made public at any rate – and of course was aware of the circumstances surrounding the young lady's conviction. Horrified, naturally. Stepped in to help.'
'But Jude's a policewoman,' Kyle spluttered. How could Bates be out and he not know? Why hadn't she contacted him? They had been ... close ... *almost* close.
'Not any more,' Stanhope said cheerily. 'Her acquittal notwithstanding the Met washed their hands of her, and being by all accounts an enterprising young woman she found herself an alternative career.'

'Doing what, exactly?' Kyle was still stunned by Stanhope's revelation. Buried memories came flooding into his mind – their return journey from Wales when he'd fallen asleep in the car she'd nicknamed the *Flying Flea;* waking to discover that she'd turned herself in … The pain came back like a hammer blow.

Stanhope looked pleased; this was clearly the reaction he'd been hoping for. He folded his arms and allowed himself a satisfied smile before answering. 'She's been working as a correspondent for a European television company. She's fluent in French, Spanish and German, so an ideal candidate for the type of person they were looking for. You didn't know about her language facility?'

'We didn't have much time for chit chat,' Kyle said, a touch testily.

'No?' Stanhope's brow creased in a collusive frown. 'Anyway, after her release she took herself off to France, and then popped up in Spain, poking around in the Almeria business. Naturally, we took an interest in her investigation, but lost track of her a few weeks back.'

'She was investigating the *bomb*?' Kyle rubbed his forehead, tried to work his discomfort into some cranial backwater where the pain might be more manageable.

'In a manner of speaking, yes. She was apparently tasked with covering Spain's latest attempt to persuade Nixon to finish a job the Americans had only partially completed in '69 – the removal of radioactive soil. But she caught the scent of something else, and…' He spread his hands and smiled ruefully. 'That's when she dropped off our radar.'

Kyle's inclination was to drive his fist into Stanhope's smug, self-satisfied face. The man from SIS knew perfectly well he wouldn't say no to his proposal, not now. He *couldn't* say no.

'I understand how you must feel, Mr Kyle.' Stanhope

evidently sensed what was going through Kyle's mind.

'Do you?' Kyle growled, bunched his fists.

'As though you've been backed into a corner?' Stanhope reprised his earlier quizzical expression.

'Quite the mind reader.' Kyle took a step towards him, but Stanhope stood his ground.

'You'll have backup. You'll have money. You'll have *work*, Mr Kyle. How *are* the finances, by the way? A police pension is hardly—'

Stanhope gasped as Kyle grabbed him by the collar and shoved him against the wall. A picture frame fell with a crack of splintered glass.

'Get out. *Now*.' Kyle held Stanhope, pinioned, for a long moment before finally releasing him and hauling the door open with such force that it dislodged a chunk of plaster from the wall behind it.

Stanhope appeared unfazed. He brushed himself down and regarded Kyle with interest, like a butterfly collector examining a particularly fascinating specimen. 'We'll speak soon,' he said, and tipped an imaginary hat.

Kyle slammed the front door behind him and stormed into the kitchen. He put the kettle on and rummaged in the cupboard for his tin of Darjeeling. In his tiny lounge, hands cupped around a hot mug, he thought about Bates.

Almost three years had passed since she'd stepped out of her car and disappeared from his life as abruptly as she'd entered it. Three years, two of which she'd spent in prison for the manslaughter of her senior, DI Patterson. He'd meant to visit, of course, but had found he couldn't face seeing her in prison garb, pale-faced and stoic as he'd known she would be, determined not to let the routine grind her down. He'd written a short note, but had torn it up as too mawkish, expressing too much hope. The manslaughter of a policeman by a fellow officer was a serious business, and the judge hadn't held back.

Kyle sipped his tea. He had no knowledge of her legal champion, this ex-colleague of the scheming Sven Jörgensen. If he had visited, he'd have learned about the appeal, would have been there for her when she'd been released. But then, he reflected, she hadn't exactly beaten a path to his door as her first priority after she got out. Quite the opposite: she'd gone abroad, put distance between herself and the White Cliffs. And who could blame her? Nothing that had happened had been her fault. She had been the wronged party in all of this. Patterson had been a predator, pure and simple, and he'd got what was coming to him.

Kyle tapped his tea cup with his fingernail. Jude Bates had never been far from his thoughts over the last three years, even though he'd tried to fill his time as best he could to forget his own predicament, to mend his heart from what had seemed like a double assault on his emotional welfare. First Rebecca's shock departure and then Bates, a brief, intense period when they'd been thrown together in pursuit of a common aim. And then, just as quickly, she too had been taken from him.

He lit a cigarette, rested his head on the antimacassar. Boredom and restlessness had been a secondary struggle over these last months. He'd filled his time as best he could, travelling the length and breadth of the UK, fell-walking, learning to sail; he had even attempted to persuade a private club that he was fit to have a crack at skydiving. They'd turned down his application on medical grounds, of course; honesty hadn't been the best policy in that endeavour.

He'd gone further afield for his next application – a small flying school in Wiltshire. A friend had furnished him with the necessary forged medical documents, and he'd been good to go. He'd enjoyed learning to fly. Although his navigational skills were questionable, he'd scraped through and eventually earned his pilot's license. Not that he could afford to get up into the blue yonder that often – it wasn't a cheap hobby – but he'd come to a casual arrangement with the school and a generous instructor whereby he could take a two-seater up every so often under the pretext of maintenance testing.

Nevertheless, the skydiving rejection rankled. He'd kicked himself afterwards that he hadn't attempted to conceal his condition, a mistake which inevitably provoked the usual morbid fascination and a series of intrusive follow-up questions: 'How do you *feel* every morning knowing that it could be your last? Surely there must be *something* the doctors can do?'

Kyle drew hard on his cigarette. He'd been tempted to take matters into his own hands, to beat the bullet fragment by choosing to end his life himself, but something always held him in check. Hope? Stubbornness? Sheer bloody-mindedness? Or just the basic, simple desire to go on living? He'd never been sure.

He crushed his cigarette into the ashtray. Problem was, he reflected, living without a purpose was no living at all. This was the spectre that chased him through each week, each month, whispering in his ear, *What are you doing, Kyle? What's the point of your life? What's the point of anything?* And, truth to tell, it was getting harder to ignore that carping, insistent voice, because he had no answer.

Until now.

He got up and began to pace the room. Stanhope, presumptuous prick though he was, had got under his skin, which had no doubt been his intention. Indeed, it had probably been the sole purpose of his visit. Kyle put on his coat and left the flat.

He needed air. He needed to think.

4

The slanting drizzle found its way behind Kyle's collar and into each unguarded gap in his clothing as he strode down familiar streets. He hardly noticed; he was back in Giza, analysing his motivation. Had he acted out of a simple desire to save himself, or to save a coach full of tourists? Or both? He could have stepped from the bus, made a last stand, taken a final bullet.

But he hadn't.

Kyle marched purposefully on, ignoring petrol-rainbow puddles, pedestrians and the near-indecipherable announcements of news vendors by the Tube station entrance – something about the Post Office Tower bomb and some disgruntled unit calling themselves the Angry Brigade. Perhaps he should join them; he was angry enough. Did anger have an upper and lower limit? What was an acceptable level of anger with which to apply?

He stopped outside his regular tobacconist, went in to buy matches and two packs of Kent cigarettes. He noticed the shopkeeper looking more morose than usual and asked him what was wrong. 'I don't suppose I'll be here much longer, Mr Kyle,' the man said glumly. 'They're only putting a bloody health warning on all tobacco products, aren't they?'

'You're kidding.' Kyle was genuinely surprised.

'*Smoking can harm your health,*' the tobacconist quoted. 'On every sodding packet. Bloody Conservative scaremongering. I blame Heath. And the damn Health Secretary.'

'Too many people enjoy smoking to just give up on the basis of a warning,' Kyle told him. 'I wouldn't worry about it. Besides, we've all got to die of something. That's what your smoking clientele will be thinking.'

The tobacconist grunted. 'Ain't that the truth. Well, Mr Kyle, I hope you're right.'

Outside, Kyle struck a Swan Vesta, sheltering the flaring match with his cupped hand. The rain had stopped but the wind was still funnelling along the high street carrying the promise of a change in the weather. He walked on, past the crumbling town hall, past the Odeon cinema which was now showing a film called *Quest for Love*, starring Joan Collins and Tom Bell, and eventually down some soaking steps and through an underground subway beneath the busy main road. Someone had graffitied a slogan on the dingy tiled wall:

Love is all
  All is Love
  It's all you've got
  So give your lot

Unlikely to trouble the Poet Laureate, but something about its simple sentiment struck a chord in Kyle's soul. He stopped short, re-read the lines once, twice…

Exiting the tunnel, he tried to recall Bates' face; her eyes, nose, strong chin. Her shoulder-length hair, and husky voice. The image was vague, as though his internal artist had received only the sketchiest information from which to create a rough, pencilled outline. She was still there, as she had been for the past three years, her memory a troubling loose end, an unsettling, dormant presence. A bus cruised by with a waft of diesel and a wave of rainwater, soaking his shoes. He barely noticed.

She was free. Had he known, would he have sought her out? He puffed hard on his Kent as he considered. By the time he arrived at his apartment, he knew the answer. Of course he would have. No question at all.

Kyle unlocked his front door, went inside and took a deep breath. He looked at his shoes and saw that they were soaked through. He shook them off and kicked them into a corner.

Stanhope's open, questioning expression hovered ghost-like in the hallway. Although physically absent, the man's persistence, like Rod Stewart's inescapable latest album, continued to play on repeat. Every picture told a story, so the title track lyric went. Kyle felt in his pocket for Stanhope's business card. It was still there, crushed behind his matches, but intact.

Jacob Stanhope.
Century House,
Westminster Bridge Road,
Lambeth,
London. Tel. 01 426 2544 Ext. 182.

Kyle went to the telephone and dialled the number.

As he'd known he would.

'Good to see you again, Mr Kyle.' Stanhope looked slightly incongruous behind a mahogany desk. His demeanour seemed more suited to lurking in doorways, or making clandestine visits to recruit unlikely spies. He joined his hands together, leaned forward and peered at Kyle between the twin towers of his brass inkstand. 'I take it you'd like to proceed?'

'Proceed? I don't even know what I'm to proceed into.'

Stanhope made a face. 'Well now, I believe I've given you an outline.'

'What you've given me is a large, fat carrot.'

'*Tch tch*. That's no way to refer to the lovely Miss Bates.'

'Careful.' Kyle growled. 'If I do this, it won't be for you, your illustrious leaders, or the British government.'

'Understood. St George to the rescue, and all that. But said love interest's disappearance may, of course, be a red herring.'

'You don't believe that.'

'What I believe is neither here nor there, Mr Kyle. But let me be clear; you'll be required to concentrate on the job in hand.'

'Namely?'

'To ensure our red-starred friends don't get their hands on that fourth explosive device Or if they do, that they don't get up to any mischief with it.'

Kyle sat back and folded his arms. 'I'm an ex-policeman. Yes, I have skills, but they're rusty and limited. You really expect me to waltz in there and deal with the KGB on my own?'

Stanhope said nothing for a few moments. When he spoke again, it was in a lower, more confidential tone. 'We find ourselves in a rather … ah, awkward situation, Mr Kyle. Under normal circumstances we would, of course, despatch a senior operative – more than one, in fact – to deal with a situation such as this.' He shrugged. 'Sadly, no such resources are currently available.'

'You have no one? Really? This is SIS, correct? MI6?'

'I can't go into detail, Mr Kyle. I can only refer to your handling of the Giza incident. According to my sources, there was scant evidence of … rust … in your handling of that particular threat.'

'As I said before, it was instinctive. That's all.'

'Then it's your instinct we're hiring, Mr Kyle.' Stanhope folded his arms and regarded Kyle as though he were an unusual but fascinating zoo animal. 'Look at it from my perspective. An ex-policeman, handy with a firearm, physically strong – rugby player, yes? – and with a certain ... shall we say *gung ho* attitude to life and survival, due to ...' He smiled, an attempt to disarm. 'Well, we needn't go into that, but you get my drift.'

Kyle parked his objections. The whys and wherefores mattered little; Bates was in trouble. That was enough. He leaned forward. 'Any suggestions where to start?'

'By the water. Look for marine activity masquerading as business-as-usual. But be discreet.'

'Where was Jude Bates staying?'

'Hotel *Casa Justa* – basic, but the only accommodation that can label itself a hotel.'

'Terms and conditions?'

'Favourable, and to follow.'

The fluorescent lights in the small office dimmed as a power fluctuation ran through the building. Kyle frowned. 'Not paid your utilities bill?'

'Happens from time to time,' Stanhope replied. 'Old building. Needs rewiring.' He pushed an envelope across the desk.

Kyle opened it. An air ticket to Almeria. Single. Stanhope anticipated his next question.

'You can make your own return arrangements – when the job's done.'

'You'll cover expenses?'

'Naturally.'

Kyle pocketed the envelope. 'I'll be in touch.'

Stanhope nodded. 'I do hope so, Mr Kyle.'

5

The late-September sun still had the strength to coax perspiration from Kyle's forehead as he trekked across the car park to the entrance of the Hotel Casa Justa. It didn't look much; it was a plain building with faded curtains and the air of a stop gap for those passing through. This wasn't one of Spain's tourist hotspots; far from it, the prevailing vibe, to coin an expression Kyle had picked up from a teenage boy on his curtailed trip to Giza, was very much a local one. Palomares still belonged to the Spanish, and they were probably grateful for it.

He pushed his way through the glazed front door and was immediately assailed by the smell of old wood mingled with the taint of grilled fish and onion. A middle-aged woman, overweight but with an open, attractive face, was seated behind the reception desk smoking a small cigarillo. Kyle felt a sudden pang of homesickness for the familiar odour of his local pub; the waft of warm, oily air preceding a tube train's arrival at Bethnal Green, the earthy scent of drizzle falling from a sky of patchwork grey. A trickle of sweat ran down his collar as he approached the desk.

'*Buenas tardes.*' A greeting lifted directly from his phrase book.

The woman nodded. '*¿Una habitación?*'

'Yes – yes, please. *Por favor.*'

'*¿Una noche, dos?*'

'I'm not sure. Let's say a week to begin with.'

'OK. *¿Periodista?*'

Journalist. Kyle shook his head; he'd prepared for this question 'No. A writer. *Escritor de bolsillo.*' A paperback writer. It seemed a reasonable cover, and it would explain why he might want to be holed up in the back of beyond for a while. '*Paz y tranquilidad.*' Peace and quiet. He smiled.

She gave him a look, returned his smile and a key attached to a rectangular wooden strip with the number twelve inscribed in faded yellow. '*Piso superior. Primero a la derecha.*'

'On the right? Thanks. *Gracias.*'

The room was unremarkable, spartan almost. A bed, bedside cabinet, a wardrobe. Plain walls, a vase of artificial flowers on top of an ancient chest of drawers. Stanhope had been accurate in his description; basic it certainly was. He found a bathroom along the corridor and splashed water on his wrists and face, returned to his room and changed his shirt. His watch told him it was five thirty-three. Time for a quick reconnaissance of the area before a bite to eat.

As he made his way downstairs to the foyer he considered the wisdom of asking the señora whether she'd seen a woman answering Bates' description. She must have stayed here, surely? There was nowhere else. And that being the case, assuming she hadn't checked out and left the area, her room might reveal something about her disappearance. But then again it was reasonable to assume that the señora would have noticed her absence, regarded it as suspicious that the lady-reporter hadn't returned to collect her belongings, and called the *Policia*. Or maybe they just didn't ask questions in Palomares. For the time being, he decided he too would follow that maxim.

As it happened, he wouldn't have had an opportunity to speak to the señora anyway. When he arrived in the lobby she had company; a man in shorts and a faded blue T-shirt was conversing with her in stilted Spanish. The woman looked uncomfortable.

Kyle kept walking but as he passed the reception desk the man turned and looked at him. It wasn't a friendly look, but Kyle doubted whether the man's battered features were capable of arranging themselves into anything remotely resembling friendly. The face was puce with sun exposure, the nose broken, the eyes small and birdlike but glinting with animal intelligence. These things Kyle noticed immediately, but it was the sheer size of the man that struck him above all else; he was enormous, well over six and a half feet, Kyle estimated, with biceps you'd be hard pushed to encircle with two hands, and pectorals bulging like slabs of meat beneath the straining material of his T-shirt. Kyle nodded and kept going.

When he reached his hire car in the hotel car park, he paused to take in the view. In the near distance the sea was calm and glinting as restless white horses caught the sun. A cargo ship moved, snail-like, across the compass line of the horizon, destination unknown. A few locals were gathered on the street outside the guest house, gesticulating and conversing as they discussed some parochial event or issue.

Kyle leaned against the car, lit a cigarette and pondered his first move. Bates could be anywhere. The enemy – should he think of them as such? – could also be nearby, or perhaps they'd moved on, abandoning their maritime project in favour of some easier mischief. How did spies think? Did they slavishly obey their masters or follow a rather more subjective and self-serving agenda while appearing to comply with their bosses' orders? He'd find out soon enough.

He suddenly had the feeling he was being observed, and

turned to see if he was right. The giant from the hotel foyer was standing by the entrance. They exchanged silent, appraising looks before the man walked briskly towards a parked motorbike, climbed astride it and roared off leaving a plume of dirty exhaust in his wake. Kyle fished the car keys from his pocket. Why not? He might learn something to his advantage. If it proved to be a false trail, so be it; he had no other plans for the evening.

It was easy to follow the motorbike. The grey fumes hung in the air like a tainted signpost, but in any case the route was straight enough. The man was headed north. As he passed a sign which read *Villaricos 1km*, Kyle eased off the throttle, felt for the gear shift on the wrong side and corrected himself with a grin. Left hand drives never felt right. He slowed to just under thirty and entered the village as the motorbike roared to a halt by a quay where a few fishing boats lay at anchor, bobbing gently as the tide slapped their hulls. Kyle parked next to a row of partially dilapidated houses that formed a protective screen around the tiny port, although it was hard to imagine bad weather on a day like today. Then he imagined Anthrax spores blowing through the village, the suffering that would result, and felt a cold chill deep in the pit of his stomach.

He lit a cigarette and watched to see where the motorbike man was headed. He didn't have to wait long; a figure appeared from the cabin of the largest fishing vessel, and gestured impatiently for the biker to come onboard. He did so, bridging the gap between the boat and the harbour side surprisingly gracefully. Both men disappeared inside.

There was nothing about this scene that could be described as out of the ordinary, nor was there much sign of life in the village. Apart from a leather-skinned old man in cutoff jeans and a dark shirt mending nets beside a mushroom-shaped bollard, the village and its environs were quiet, sleepy almost, under the balmy evening sky.

But the big guy looked wrong. Kyle puffed on his cigarette, lowered the window and flicked ash. Not a tourist. Not a fisherman. Not a local.

The boat's engine fired, failed, fired again and caught. Kyle's person of interest reappeared on deck and untied the moorings. Kyle watched as the boat slowly turned and pointed its prow out to sea leaving a bubbling wake behind. It looked way too small to be a salvage vessel, but maybe there was such a bigger craft already in situ at the recovery site, and maybe the small fishing boat was being used to ferry those involved to and fro.

Maybe.

Kyle finished his cigarette, shoved the gearstick into first and executed a neat three point turn. At least now he had a starting point. Motorbike man was up to something, and his gut told him it had very little to do with fish.

6

The proprietress was standing outside the guesthouse, smoking and looking anxious. Kyle's return elicited a forced smile and a polite *buenas noches, señor* as he went in. He still wanted to ask her about Bates but he was tired and hungry and needed a shower. His current headache was bearable, somewhere around two and a half on the scale and experience had taught him that hot water and food sometimes helped to take the edge off.

He passed an elderly woman in the corridor who ignored his greeting and continued on her way, muttering under her breath. Maybe they just didn't like English people in Palomares. American distrust? He could understand that – after all, the Yanks had come close to removing the entire area from the map. He glanced left and right outside his room but there was no one else around. He unlocked the door and went in. And stopped dead.

'Hello, Kyle.'

Jude Bates was sitting on his bed, smoking what appeared to be a small Spanish cigarillo.

'Sorry. Bit of a surprise, I expect.' Bates exhaled, stubbed out the cigarillo, smiled and rose to her feet.

Kyle found his voice. 'You could say.'

'Hope you don't mind my borrowing your room. I was trying to avoid someone.'

'Big guy, cropped blond hair?'

'That's the one.'

'Gone fishing,' Kyle said, recovering some of his composure. 'Or put to sea, at any rate.'

'That figures.' She folded her arms and looked at him. It was a look he remembered. Appraising, challenging.

Kyle wondered if he should offer his hand, or maybe kiss her on the cheek, but felt like that moment had passed. Instead he jammed his hands into his trouser pockets. 'Well it's good to see that you haven't been kidnapped or murdered at least.'

'Is that what Stanhope told you?'

Kyle shook his head wearily. He was too tired for guessing games. 'I think it might be helpful if you just explained what you're up to.'

She went to the window and looked out. 'I thought you might have visited, back in England. Or written, maybe.'

He had no answer.

'Oh well,' she went on after a moment. 'I was obviously hoping for too much.'

'I *did* mean to—'

'It doesn't matter now, Kyle. You have your own problems, I get it.'

'I'm all right. It's just—'

She turned, looked him up and down. 'You've lost weight.'

'Food's never interested me that much.' Kyle pulled a towel from his open suitcase and rummaged for his toiletries. Any residual adrenaline that had kept him going had been replaced by a heavy weariness. Bates was safe, apparently well. He'd been misled. The whys and wherefores could wait, but her evasiveness irritated him. 'I'm going for a shower.'

'Good luck. The plumbing is positively prehistoric.'

'I'll take my chances. And don't light another of those bloody Spanish fireworks while I'm gone.'

She was right about the plumbing. That, too, was irritating. But as the lukewarm water spurted sporadically over his naked body, Kyle's anger slowly dissipated. Whatever was going on in Palomares didn't involve – or hadn't yet involved – Bates coming to harm. He should be grateful for that. Now he had got over the shock of her sudden appearance, he realised he'd missed her more than he'd been willing to admit. Maybe that was why he'd never visited her in Holloway – it would have been too painful to see her incarcerated, to experience the reality of her imprisonment.

He towel-dried his hair and made his way back to his room. Bates was lying on the bed, eyes closed. As he shut the door behind him she opened them. 'Better?'

He grunted. 'Clean, at any rate.'

'Look, Kyle, I understand why you're annoyed.' She sat up, swung her feet onto the floor and stretched. 'I dozed off for a minute there. It's the heat.'

'You understand why I might be a little put out that I've travelled all the way from England to Spain on the false pretext that you were missing, perhaps in danger? Only to find you fit and well and kipping on my bed? Why on earth should I be put out by that?'

'Oh, Kyle. You haven't changed, have you?' She approached him and took the towel from him, threw it onto the bed. 'Still as stroppy as ever.' She held his arms lightly. 'I knew you'd be all right. And I knew you'd come. I'm sorry for the subterfuge, really I am.'

He stared dumbly into her eyes. There was a tiny scar on her forehead, just above her right eyebrow. It was new. He wanted to kiss it.

'Hurry up and get dressed,' she said, releasing his arms. 'There's a nice little tapas bar around the corner. I'll treat you.

You need feeding up.'

'Only if you tell me what you're playing at.'

'Playing? I'm not playing, Kyle. But I do promise to tell you what I know.'

The bar was almost empty, apart from a couple of local workers downing strong drink in a corner and a dozing dog by the entrance awning.

'This does look inviting,' Kyle said.

'The food is better than the ambience, trust me.' Bates walked confidently to the counter and greeted a swarthy man in a grubby apron with a stream of Spanish Kyle didn't bother trying to follow. He remembered Stanhope's assessment of Bates' linguistic abilities. *Hidden depths...*

They were directed to a table beneath the awning. The waiter brought them a jug, two glasses and a hand-written menu.

After giving the dense lettering a swift look, Kyle said, 'I have no idea what any of this is, so I'll leave the ordering to you.' He poured a measure of the reddish liquid from the jug into Bates' glass. 'I have no idea what this is, either.'

Bates chuckled. 'Sangria. You'll like it.' She took a sip and smacked her lips. 'It means *bloodletting.*'

'Of course it does.' Kyle filled his own glass and took a sip. It wasn't as bad as he'd expected.

The waiter returned with a pen, a clipboard and a quizzical expression. Again, Kyle didn't bother to follow the conversation.

Bates sipped sangria and gave him the look again, the same as before. It made it hard for him to collect his thoughts, and harder still to stay angry.

'Spill the beans, Bates. The suspense is killing me.'

'All right. So, while I was inside I had a lot of time to think. About my life, what I was going to do with it after I got out. I was going to travel, Kyle. See the world. The last thing I wanted to do was stay in England, after what had happened.'

Kyle drank sangria and listened.

'I had no idea that someone was championing my case. None at all. First I knew was when he came to visit.'

'Peter Wiltshire?'

'Stanhope told you? OK, yes, him.'

The waiter reappeared with a tray and set it down. Kyle failed to identify the contents of the dishes he arranged before them, but they smelled good. He hadn't realised how hungry he was and felt himself salivating.

'*Gracias.*' Bates smiled sweetly at the waiter and gestured to Kyle. 'Tuck in.'

She went on, 'So, Peter was lovely. And confident, very confident. He knew exactly which prosecution weaknesses could be exploited on appeal. He teased them out, saw the appeal process through and represented me in court himself.'

'Quite a guy.' Kyle picked a sample from his plate and took a bite. 'Not bad. What is it?'

'Chorizo. It's a sausage. And that's squid.' She jabbed her fork at Kyle's next target.

'I might pass on that one.'

'It's good. Don't be so bloody English.' She forked a morsel into her mouth by way of example and chewed it appreciatively.

Kyle picked up his glass. 'And then?'

'And then … I was out. And a day later, Peter asked me to dinner.'

Kyle's glass broke in his hand. Sangria splashed freely over the tablecloth, his trousers. '*Shit!*' He instinctively scraped his chair back, almost pulling the tablecloth with him. 'Sorry, sorry—'

The owner arrived, all flapping hands and soothing noises. Having assessed the damage, he promptly returned with damp cloths and a new tablecloth. A younger waiter appeared, cleared their meal from the table, laid a fresh tablecloth and reinstated plates, two fresh glasses and the remains of the tapas. A new jug of sangria magically appeared and was laid gently upon the new diorama with a practised flourish.

'*Muchas gracias,*' Bates said.

'*Es un placer, señora.*'

'Sorry about that,' Kyle muttered.

Again, the look. 'I didn't know you cared, Kyle. Anyway, as I was saying, Peter was charming, as always, but this time he had an ulterior motive. He wanted to introduce me to someone.'

Now Kyle could see what was coming and he felt even more stupid than before. 'They recruited you. Stanhope and co.'

'He and Peter are old friends,' Bates said. 'They were at Eton together.'

'Of course they were.' Kyle poured himself a generous slug of sangria. He looked into her eyes and raised an eyebrow. 'A correspondent for a European television company, that's what Stanhope told me. I wonder, did your boss tell me *anything* that might roughly correspond to the truth? No pun intended.'

Bates shrugged. 'Look, like I said, I'm sorry for all the cloak and dagger stuff, but it was important to get you here, by whatever means.'

'Important for whom?'

'For *me*, you idiot. Who do you think?'

He was momentarily flabbergasted. 'What? I don't—'

Bates leaned across the table and lowered her voice to a whisper. 'Yes, he *did* tell you the truth – about the most important thing; about the bomb, the threat, the soviet operation. I bet he told you there was no one else available, am I right?'

Kyle nodded.

'That's because they killed the agent I've been working with, Kyle,' she hissed. 'That's why I wanted an urgent replacement. That's why I needed support.'

Now they were almost nose to nose, but she leaned in even closer and chucked him under the chin. '*That's* why I asked for you.'

7

Kyle put his glass down carefully, slowly. 'Let me get this straight. Stanhope recruited you and then you recruited me?'

'I can think of worse jobs.' She shrugged and nibbled on a chunk of chorizo.

Kyle reflected for a moment. 'I came for you. You're OK. I should walk out of here right now. Just go home.'

'Come on. Kyle. To do what? Sit around feeling sorry for yourself?'

That hit the button. He felt his face redden. 'That is *entirely* unfair. You've got a bloody nerve, Bates.' He stood and slammed his glass down, drawing a worried look from the older waiter. 'If you want to swan around saving the world, fine, that's up to you. I didn't ask for this. I came here because I thought you were in trouble.' He was aware that his voice had risen to an inappropriate level and struggled for control, glaring at the two waiters who were both staring in their direction.

'Calm it, Kyle.' She refilled his glass. 'And keep your voice down. I don't want to attract unwarranted attention. You're here now, you might as well hear me out.'

Kyle shuffled his feet. 'I do *not* feel sorry for myself.'

'OK. I take it back. But be honest, what's in London for you these days?'

She had a point; he just didn't want to concede it. 'And what exactly do you know about my life?'

'Enough.'

'You and your Eton buddies have been spying on me, is that it?'

'Did you expect your Giza heroics to go unnoticed?' She picked up his glass and offered it.

'I wasn't expecting anything. I was on holiday.'

'Stop being such an arse, Kyle. Here. Take your drink. Park your bum.'

Defeated, he sat down again and accepted the sangria.

She lowered her voice again. 'You saved a bus full of tourists from being shot. It was a remarkable performance.'

'I acted on pure instinct. You'd have done the same.'

'I'm not sure I would've, I'm really not.'

He swigged sangria. 'Whatever.'

'So, will you?'

'Will I what?'

'Hear me out.'

'I suppose.'

'Good.' Bates selected a morsel of squid and popped it in her mouth. 'OK, this is where we're at—'

Kyle held up both hands, palms out. 'Wait. How can you be doing this?' He looked at her with something close to amazement. 'You're so calm about it all, like you've been working for SIS all your life.' A thought occurred to him. 'You haven't, have you?'

'Don't be daft. 'Course not. I really was a policewoman, Kyle. You saw that first hand.'

He grudgingly conceded the point.

She leaned forward again. 'I had a seriously unpleasant time inside, Kyle. I can't tell you. You can only really appreciate what freedom is when you've experienced what

I've experienced.'

'I don't doubt it.'

She pursed her lips, fell silent for a moment.

Kyle waited.

Eventually she sighed. 'This is hard for me.'

'Take your time.'

She flashed a weak smile, drew a long breath. Her fingers tapped out a rhythm on her cigarillos pack. 'I seriously thought about ... well, about killing myself, afterwards. You know what they say – mud sticks. I was fully exonerated, sure, but in reality people still look at you and think: she's a killer.'

'I'm sorry. Give it time.'

'Yeah, right. What was I supposed to do? Travel, yes, OK. But that was never going to be enough.'

'So ... you needed something to work out, what? Your anger?'

A shrug. 'Maybe. I didn't go looking for it, though. It came to me.'

'In the shape of Stanhope.' Kyle prodded a cold piece of chorizo, thought better of it, and put his fork down.

'He's all right. I've met worse.'

'Jury's out on that.'

'So are you going to help me or not?' She rested her elbows on the table and joined her hands, fingers interlaced.

'How can I say no?'

That brought a smile to her lips. 'Thank you. May I continue?'

Kyle turned to check on the waiters. The bar was beginning to fill up and they were both busy attending to other tables. 'If you think it's safe.'

'It's safe. Just be vigilant.'

'What am I looking for? Large men with cropped hair?'

'Definitely that. Anything that looks wrong.'

'So far, pretty much everything here looks wrong.'

She laughed. 'You know what I mean. I trust your instincts; you should, too. I reckon they're pretty good, if Giza's anything to go by.'

'Can we forget Giza?'

'I won't mention it again.'

'I'll hold you to that.' Kyle grunted, lit a cigarette. 'So, go ahead. I'm all ears.'

She nodded, leaned forward conspiratorially. 'Stanhope will have told you the essentials. The intelligence is correct. We have a red operation here and so far I've identified five persons of interest.'

'Now you sound like DC Bates.' He blew smoke.

'Old habits. What can I say?' She gave a short, self-deprecating chuckle. 'A mile or so offshore there's an operation underway to salvage the warhead. You already know what it contains, and why they have to be stopped.'

'How do you know they haven't secured it already?'

'I just do. If you want to know, a colleague found a way to message me.'

'This colleague is, presumably, close to the action?'

Bates hesitated. 'He was.'

'Ah. The lost asset.'

Bates looked down at her plate.

'Sorry. Sore point, I imagine.'

Bates' eyes were still fixed on her plate, the table cloth. 'I blame myself, Kyle. I should have stopped him.'

A waiter appeared and efficiently cleared the table. '¿Otro trago?'

Kyle frowned.

'Another drink?' Bates translated.

Kyle shook his head. The sangria had crossed the boundary and his headache had clicked over to a four or five.

'Nosotros estamos bien, gracias.'

Kyle ground his cigarette into the ashtray. 'Shall we continue somewhere more private?' The bar was getting busy; families had begun to arrive and the volume of conversation was escalating, frequently interspersed with the demanding shrills of small children. He grimaced as a particularly loud yell rose above the hubbub. 'My head may not survive a lengthy conversation.'

'Sure. Let me get the bill.' Bates pushed her chair back and went to the counter. Kyle watched her as she manoeuvred between tables, children and fussing parents. She'd lost weight too, but seemed fit and toned. Her hair was shorter than he remembered, lighter, her neck the deepest shade of brown. She'd been *in situ* a while.

The roar of a motorbike engine caught his attention. He glanced to his right just as a flashbulb went off in his face. Bates was at his side as he leaped to his feet. The motorbike engine screamed as the rider turned a full one-eighty and accelerated away.

'Thought you said it was safe?' Kyle glared as exhaust fumes stung his nostrils.

'It was a camera, Kyle, not a gun. If they'd wanted you dead, you would be.' She took his arm and they hurried away along the narrow street. 'It's their way of saying hi, we know you're here.'

'I don't find that particularly comforting.'

'It's what they do. No one can stay incognito for long, not in a place like this.'

The night was warm and the peaceful sound of the sea murmuring against the shoreline was at odds with the tension Kyle was feeling. He was suddenly overcome with a sense of unreality, as though he'd dreamed the past twenty-four hours. He stopped, leaned against a low wall by a row of Spanish *casas*.

'Are you OK?'

'Just my head. Give me a moment.'

She folded her arms, gazed out to sea. 'It's all happening out there. We haven't much time.'

He closed his eyes, blinked, and his head cleared a fraction. 'You'd better tell me the rest, then. Your place or mine?'

'Mine. The señora has given me a room in the basement, in the guesthouse *privado* area.'

'Taken a shine to you, has she?'

'No. But she's seen who's interested in checking me out. Her idea. I thought it prudent to accept. I left a few things in my original room to throw interested parties off the scent.'

They passed beneath a plane tree, in the sparse foliage of which some agitated bird was shrilling a late evening call.

To Kyle, it sounded like a warning.

The room was warm, the open shutters providing occasional wafts of air that seemed only to circulate the heat, move it around from one area to the next. Bates sat on the iron bedstead, Kyle on a wooden chair in front of the worn dresser whose cracked mirror reflected the tired lines beneath his eyes as he took in his new surroundings. He quickly glanced away, focused on Bates, an altogether more pleasing prospect. He could feel an steady pulse in his temple tolling like a muted bell.

'You look like crap, Kyle.'

'I'll be fine after a few hours kip.'

'OK, I'll keep this short – and by the way, I wouldn't go back to your room.'

He frowned, and she rolled her eyes.

'Don't get excited. There's an old camp bed stashed behind the wardrobe. I'll sleep on that.'

He raised a hand to object but she cut him off. 'Your need is greater.'

Too tired to argue, he waved acquiescence.

'So.' Bates ran a hand through her short cut. 'Like I said earlier, our POIs have established the whereabouts of the item in question. The boat you saw is the taxi to the site. They've got a larger vessel at anchor which has all the necessary bells and whistles to salvage the object of interest. But they've run into problems.'

'What sort of problems?'

'Practical. The object moved. There was a storm two days ago; not the worst, but bad enough. They had to up sticks and sit it out onshore, and when they got back to the original co-ordinates they discovered that said object was sitting on the edge of a fissure.'

'And now?' Kyle scratched his chin.

'Now they have to figure out how to salvage it without tipping it over the edge. If they do, it's going down another thirty or forty fathoms where it'll be pretty much unsalvageable.'

'I'm not familiar with jolly jack tar weights and measures. How deep exactly is a fathom?'

'Around six feet. Do the maths.'

'OK. Yeah, that's a problem, for sure.'

'Yep.'

'So, assuming they do manage to raise it, what are we going to do with it? Roll it up the beach and drive it to London?'

Bates came over and put her face an inch from his nose. 'They won't get that far. We're going to finish what the storm began. We're going to nudge that warhead right into the fissure.'

The net curtain fluttered and a shadow moved into the square of light cast by the ceiling bulb onto the paved area outside the window. Kyle grabbed Bates around the waist and dragged her onto the floor just as a small, round object rolled across the worn linoleum. Shielding a protesting Bates with his body, he upended the bed frame and curled himself around her.

The grenade exploded with a muted thump and the room was plunged into darkness. Shrapnel pinged against the metal bedframe and tore into the mattress with the sound of ripping cloth. The room filled with the stink of explosive. Kyle felt Bates' fingernails in his back as a motorbike engine roared, tyres screeched, the noise of its engine fading into a familiar doppler tail-off.

Bates coughed, relaxed her vice-like grip on his torso. Kyle shoved the bed frame aside and peered out. Plaster fragments covered the floor along with shards of mirror glass and rags of Bates' clothing. Her suitcase was upended in a corner, studded with metal. Foul yellow smoke hung in the air like the remnant of a gas attack.

Kyle jammed his handkerchief over his mouth and crawled to his feet, checked himself up and down. No blood. Bates emerged on her haunches, levered herself upright but immediately doubled over again, racked with a fusillade of coughing.

'Might I suggest alternative accommodation?' Kyle opened the door, intact apart from a splintered shrapnel scar next to the handle. The señora must have heard, surely? But there was no sign of her in the corridor.

Kyle took Bates' hand and they exited the room, heading through the *privado* door and into the lobby. The señora had not heard. She was lolling at the reception desk, a neat hole in her forehead. A single rivulet of blood tracked down to her right eye where it pooled and stained her over-rouged cheek.

Bates hesitated, her expression stricken. Kyle pulled her arm. '*Come on,*' he hissed. 'It's too late for her and definitely not safe for us.'

He gestured urgently behind them, to where fire was already spreading into the hall from Bates' wrecked bedroom into the *privado* corridor.

She came, reluctantly. '*Bastardos.*' She spat the word as they emerged into the car park, coughing to clear the smoke stuck in her throat.

'My sentiments exactly,' Kyle said. He led her towards his hired car but she pulled away. 'Not safe.'

'Then what?'

'Just follow me.'

She began walking along the road, away from the guest house, turned to check he was following. Kyle sighed, fell into step. Sleep would have to wait.

8

The harbourside apartment was small, airless. There was one living room, one bedroom, a tiny kitchenette. a cubby-hole toilet with a dysfunctional shower jammed into the corner as an afterthought. It had belonged to an old fisherman, long dead, and the place had lain derelict for years. The rooms smelled of stale fish and tobacco.

If this, Alek Yurichenko thought bitterly, was the standard of accommodation his betters considered appropriate for someone of his seniority, then it must call into question the nature of the promised 'great reward' he'd been told to expect on his triumphant return to the Motherland. He took an irritated pull at his cigarette. Perhaps he would have coped better had he not been obliged to share the hovel with his subordinate, who had developed the annoying habit of positioning himself at the window and making pointless remarks about every local, bicyclist, or gaggle of youths passing along the quayside.

Oleg Gordiovski was a big man – a ruffian, in Yurichenko's view, but an ambitious and powerful one. He had, Yurichenko knew, friends in high places; the army, navy, and most tellingly, the shadowy corridors of the Kremlin.

He'd built a solid reputation on his ability to identify and remove threats, to protect a mission. That's why he was here. Gordiovski didn't know the meaning of the words *circumspect, tact* or *diplomacy*; he was ruthless, without scruples, and the two men had arrived at an uneasy alliance, its fragile balance maintained only by Yurichenko's seniority.

'That bloody drunk again.' Gordiovski snorted in disdain. From outside, the faint strains of a slurred sentimental song bounced around the stone and concrete of the harbour.

'He'll fall in one day, drown himself.' Gordiovski abandoned his post and headed for the kitchenette to refill his glass.

'You're sure you weren't followed?' Yurichenko intercepted Gordiovski's progress with a raised hand.

'Not followed.'

'They're both dead? The woman *and* the new arrival?'

'Yes.'

'Good. Miss Bates' allegiances were highly suspect. Any other damage?'

'The cow that ran the place.' Gordiovski gave a harsh laugh.

'I suppose that was absolutely necessary?' Yurichenko sighed. He knew that Gordiovski enjoyed his work, maybe too much. They couldn't afford to be careless. Not now.

'She was a nosy bitch.'

That was enough justification, in Gordiovski's mind. Yurichenko heard his comrade rooting around in the cupboard for the vodka bottle.

'You drink too much,' Yurichenko said.

'Mind your own business.'

'Mind your own business, *sir*.'

'Whatever.'

Yurichenko gritted his teeth, but he was keenly aware that there was little to be gained by trying to enforce the respect due to his seniority. Gordiovski would do what he was told –

up to a point, and usually only when confronted with the repercussions if he refused, not that repercussions had ever bothered Gordiovski in the past. Yurichenko had given up trying to earn the giant's respect; that wasn't going to happen. The best he could do was hope to control him until they were done – which would be soon, very soon. Then he could get out of this shit hole and make his move.

Yurichenko shivered in spite of the temperature. *His move.* It sounded innocuous, but his plan was fraught with risks. He stiffened his shoulders. He would face what was coming, what he had to do, come hell or high water. Maybe, he reflected, both options would apply.

Gordiovski emerged from the kitchen clutching the vodka bottle which, Yurichenko noticed, was now two thirds empty. He knew from experience that a drunk Gordiovski was much worse than the sober version. The man became more irrational, more liable to bouts of moodiness, even anger – and right now there was only one place he could direct that anger. But Gordiovski needed to be reminded who was in charge, and it was also a good idea to keep him busy. Yurichenko took a breath. 'The Spaniard. Think he needs a little incentive to stay on board with us?'

Gordiovski sloshed vodka into a dirty glass and threw it back. He smacked his lips and nodded. 'Da. He's flaky.'

Yurichenko raised an eyebrow. 'Americanisms now, Gordy? You have been practising without my knowledge?'

Gordiovski glared at him, then growled, 'You're messing with me, *Kapitan.*'

'A joke, Gordy.'

'We'll take the girl. That should do it.'

Yurichenko considered the suggestion. They would need somewhere to keep her. Not here – too exposed, and too cramped. He stubbed his cigarette out on the heel of his boot. Their support vessel, a RVK-1148, was due at the coordinates of the warhead by five, just before dawn. If they could get the girl on board the *Tronio*, their hired fishing boat, by say, four, then they could transfer her to the larger vessel before the village woke up. Yurichenko mulled the idea over. He couldn't see a problem. 'OK, yes, do it. But—' Yurichenko wagged a warning finger. 'No bloodshed, and leave the wife alone. Tell the Spaniard that his blossom will be fine if he continues to assist us. She will be returned to him when our job is complete.'

'I'll be right back.' A grinning Gordiovski was already at the door, his small eyes glinting at the prospect of inflicting pain, albeit emotional rather than physical.

'I'll be waiting,' Yurichenko said. 'In the boat. So don't be late. And don't screw it up.'

'Ah, so I am not the only one practising his Americanisms, eh? *Sir*.'

The door closed with a bang and Yurichenko was alone. He allowed himself to relax, a luxury only possible in Gordiovski's absence.

9

Bates led Kyle along the coastal road until they reached a turning. A sign pointed inland to a place Kyle didn't recognise – not that he'd recognised any town or Spanish village since his arrival, apart from Palomares itself. He called to her as she turned right, following the narrow inland road.

'Please tell me we're close to wherever we're going.'

'It's just along here.'

'What is?'

'A friend's house.'

'They'd better be friendly – you're aware of the time?'

'It'll be all right, Kyle. They're night owls here.'

She stopped outside a single-storey house with a postage-stamp front garden. There was, of course, no grass, just a few pots with sparse green shoots – cacti, maybe – positioned here and there atop a shallow layer of pebbles. A canopy of blossoming bougainvillea overarched the garden like a colourful umbrella. Bates strode up to the front door and knocked.

A light flickered on inside, a key scraped in the lock and the front door opened, the doorway framing a man in his mid-forties. He was wearing a white singlet and a pair of khaki shorts.

'*Buenas noches, Francisco, siento molestarte a estas horas.*'

The man grinned, held the door open. '*No hay problema, señorita Judy, por favor entre.*' He gave a short nod to Kyle. '*Señor.*'

They were shown into a small lounge, simply furnished in typical Spanish style. The wall was decorated with two large paintings, one depicting the harbour at Villaricos, but many years ago by the look of it, and the other a fishing boat in the open sea. A narrow archway, framed by a string of coloured seashells, led into a short corridor where Kyle supposed the bedrooms and bathroom were located. A woman with long, dark hair hovered in the background next to a small kitchenette; at Francisco's soft request she immediately set to work with a light clattering of pans and clinking of glassware.

'Please. Sit.' Francisco indicated the two armchairs. Kyle gratefully sank into the nearest.

Bates caught a glimpse of herself in the glass of the back door, brushed herself down. 'I'm sorry to disturb you like this, Francisco. I didn't know where else to go.'

Francisco nodded.

Kyle caught her eye and Bates got the unspoken question.

'This is Francisco. He found the first missing H-bomb, the one that hit the seabed. He's a fisherman and he knows these waters better than I know the ceiling plaster cracks in my prison cell. He helped Uncle Sam with the salvage op.'

Kyle raised his hand in greeting. '*Hola.*' To Bates, he said, 'Any English?'

'A little.' *Sotto voce* she added, 'His wife's name is Arianna. Hers is better.'

Francisco was eying them both, a worried expression creasing his weathered face. '*¿Estáis heridos?*'

'He's asking if we're hurt.' She shook her head. '*No, estamos bien*'

'We probably smell like a Guy Fawkes bonfire.'

She laughed at that. 'You could literally double as the guy, Kyle.'

It was true. They were both covered in soot, dirt and plaster dust. Bates' hair was awry and Kyle's shirt was torn.

Arianna placed a tray on the dining table, indicated they should help themselves.

Francisco still wore his worried expression. Bates elaborated. *'Una granada. Los rusos'.*

Kyle got that. *Los rusos.* The bad guys.

Arianna exchanged an anxious look with her husband.

Bates reached out and squeezed Arianna's arm. *'No nos siguieron. Está bien.'*

'What are you telling them?'

'That we weren't followed. That they're safe.'

Francisco grunted. *'Comed, bebed. Estáis con amigos ahora.'*

Bates' face creased in a weary grin. 'He says, eat, drink, you are with friends now.'

Kyle tensed as a movement beneath the archway caught his attention, then relaxed again as a small girl stepped shyly into the room. She was clutching a well-worn rag doll to her chest, her large sleepy brown eyes focusing first on Kyle, then Bates, and then Arianna.

'Camila!' Arianna went to the girl, put an arm over her shoulder and whispered in her ear. Kyle estimated her age at nine or maybe ten. She was still staring at him, so he rewarded her with a smile and a wink.

'Hola, Camila.' Bates stroked Camila's hair. *'¿No duermes?'*

Arianna was still fussing over her daughter, but the girl was too curious to be ushered away without some form of explanation. Arianna whispered a few hushed, soothing words of reassurance before escorting her daughter away with an apologetic shrug.

'She's lovely,' Kyle said to Francisco, and Bates translated. *'Bonita.'*

Francisco nodded, pulled a small, understated smile from his weather-beaten face. *'Realmente*. But she has ... *problema medico*. She is...' He searched for the word.

Bates supplied it. 'Diabetic. But she copes, right Francisco?'

'Si. Diabética.' He shrugged. *'Ella está bien.'*

'She's a little trooper. Bright, too – top of her class in maths and languages.' Bates grinned. 'I'm going to talk with Francisco now, Kyle. Bear with.'

'Fine. Go ahead.' Kyle settled himself in the armchair and soon gave up trying to follow the conversation. Francisco was nodding, seemingly in agreement with what Bates was telling him. He left the room briefly and returned with what appeared to be a nautical map, which he spread out on the table, pushing items of crockery and cutlery impatiently aside. They bent their heads over it and the conversation resumed, Francisco jabbing his finger emphatically on the paper from time to time and soliciting Bates' opinion with quick, darting movements of his head.

Through the rapid fire of their conversation, Kyle could hear Arianna speaking quietly to her daughter in another room. He felt his eyes beginning to close. His thoughts became jumbled, intertwined. The sound of Bates' and Francisco's voices receded into some distant dimension where his consciousness could not follow.

He slept.

He awoke with a start. He was still sitting in the same chair, but a blanket had been placed over him and the room was dark and silent. No, not quite silent – he could hear a soft, regular sighing from the opposite side of the room. He squinted, encouraging his night vision to identify the source. A figure, unmistakably Bates, was lying on her back on the sofa, her arm trailing carelessly on the floor and her chest rising and falling slowly in the easy rhythm of slumber. Kyle felt his muscles relax.

What had woken him? He had no idea of the time; there was no timepiece to refer to, either on the wall or on his wrist, but his instincts told him it was the stillest hour of the night, the hour just before dawn.

And then he heard a noise, a surreptitious tap, as though a lock was being tested, or a window eased open. Not this room, not the front door. He got to his feet, padded across the cool tiles until he was beneath the archway of the interconnecting hall, and listened.

Again came the sound; a subtle scraping against stone, and then ... a sharp *clack* of some secure restraint giving way to a superior force. Kyle padded forward, stopped outside a door which stood an inch or so ajar. He peered in. Two sleeping forms in a double bed; Francisco and his wife. Kyle moved on to the next, either the bathroom or the daughter's bedroom.

The bathroom.

A muffled sound, almost immediately quashed, propelled him towards the next doorway. This bedroom door was wide open. A shadow flicked across the square of the window, a large, almost ungainly form, its movements incongruously graceful, giving an impression of great strength coupled with exceptional agility.

Kyle crouched, lowering his profile, and crept into the room. The shadow was gone, the bedcovers thrown back, the bed empty. In an instant he was at the window. A few metres along the lane an engine purred into life. Lights moved rapidly away, the sound rapidly fading as the car put distance between itself and the cottage.

The noise had awakened the household. Bates appeared, bleary-eyed, closely followed by Francisco in a silk dressing gown, rapid-firing questions Kyle couldn't understand. Last came Arianna, wailing at Kyle's shoulder as the realisation set in that Camila was missing. In her hand she held a roughly scribbled note. They all automatically repaired to the living room, Francisco pulling on a pair of worn trousers, heavy boots, still shooting unintelligible questions at Bates, his wife.

'What does it say, Arianna?' Bates asked gently.

Stifling her sobs Arianna read,

I have work for Francisco. Eight o'clock by the harbour. Do not fail to show up if you care about the child.

Francisco grabbed a set of keys from a hook by the front door, made to go outside. Arianna clung to him. 'No, *por favor*, Francisco. *No!*'

'*Tranquila, tranquila!*' Bates held up both hands. Then a quick aside to Kyle, 'He wants to go after them. He has a motorbike.'

Shaking his wife off, Francisco went into another room and reappeared clutching what looked like an antiquated rifle.

'What the hell is that?' Kyle looked at Bates.

Francisco held the gun up for inspection.

'A Lee-Enfield,' Bates said. 'Probably from the civil war. Francisco, no – you can't use this. It is too dangerous.' She lowered the barrel with a gentle push so that it was pointing at the floor.

'More likely to do him harm than anyone he's pointing it at,' Kyle said.

Bates took her friend by the arm. 'No guns, Francisco, no.'

Reluctantly Francisco ejected the five-round charger and put the gun away. It took them a while to calm him, but the Spaniard eventually succumbed to reason and collapsed on the sofa, his face a mask of misery. Arianna left the room, Kyle assumed to dress and to weep in private – and pray, too, in all likelihood, if the religious icons and paintings dotted around the cottage were anything to go by.

'Coffee, I think,' Bates said. Kyle followed her into the kitchen.

'Camila's collateral,' Kyle said quietly as they stood together. 'I'm assuming our friend Francisco has been recruited to assist our Soviet buddies in their salvage op?'

Bates nodded as she fiddled around searching for mugs, coffee, teaspoons. 'He helped the Yanks locate the H-bomb warhead. He knows these waters backwards.'

'Uh huh. Was tempted by red offer at first but now decided he wants out? How am I doing?'

'Yep, you've got it.'

'And you have a plan?' Kyle rubbed his eyes.

Bates handed him two mugs of steaming coffee. 'You look like you need this. The black one's for Francisco. A plan? Not yet.' She shook her head. 'Working on it.'

They repaired to the lounge and there was silence while they drank their coffee, until eventually Francisco's patience expired. He stood up again and began to pace the room, berating the abductors and bemoaning his involvement with the Russian *cerdos*, appealing to Kyle and Bates for guidance.

'Francisco, *ella estará bien*. She will be well.' Bates spoke urgently. 'We will find her. You must go at the appointed time, do what they say.'

Arianna's tear-streaked face appeared at last from the bathroom. She had tried to make herself presentable for her guests and Kyle's heart went out to her for the effort she had made.

'We can work together, Francisco,' Bates said again. '*Juntos*.' And then to Kyle. 'You sure they didn't see you?'

'Very unlikely. It was dark, he was half way out the window. It was the same guy – the one at the hotel. No question.'

Bates nodded. 'So in all likelihood, they still think we're dead. That's an advantage.'

'For certain. Careless, too. That's another advantage. They should have made sure of us at the hotel.'

Bates gave a terse nod. 'Are we all agreed Francisco should play along?'

Arianna translated for her husband but Francisco bristled.

'*Por el bien de nuestra hija,*' Arianna took her husband's arm, eyes pleading.

'For our daughter's sake,' Bates translated for Kyle's benefit.

Francisco swallowed hard, nodded. 'OK.'

'We won't be far behind, Arianna,' Bates squeezed Arianna's shoulder. 'I promise.'

Kyle finished the dregs of his coffee. It hadn't made him feel much better. To Bates he said, 'Sorry if I'm being pedantic but before we all rush off into the great watery unknown, you'd better fill me in. Like I said, my seafaring knowledge begins and ends with candy floss on Southend Pier.'

'I hear you, Kyle.' She motioned for them all to gather round. '*Escuchen atentamente.* This is what we're going to do.'

10

Una chica inteligente…
… chica inteligente …

This, Camila decided, would be her mantra. Her papá had said it, her mama had said it. She was a clever girl. It was time to prove it to herself, and to *sus padres …*

She was frightened, but not as much as she thought she might be. Camila was a practical girl, a top scorer in mathematics, languages, and reading at school. When she realised that the big man meant her no immediate harm, she did her best to consider her situation in a way that any grown up would consider to be a very mature manner. These people wanted Papa to help them do something bad, and Papa would not. She had heard *sus padres* discussing it in hushed, urgent voices after she'd gone to bed and was supposed to be asleep. The bad men, *los Rojos*, Papa always called them, they were here because of the bombs that had fallen on the land and in the sea – although that had been *los Americanos'* fault, the soldiers she had seen scouring the countryside after the big bang in the sky when people had died in the air.

But *los Rojos* – well, they were planning something mean, something even worse than the aeroplane accident, she knew that much. And they wanted Papa to help. And he wouldn't. And now they'd stolen her from Papa and he would be made to do bad things with them.

Camila wasn't going to let that happen. Papa was Papa. He was famous, the man who had found the missing bomb in the sea. He had done a fine thing for *los Americanos*, stopped another bad accident happening. *Los Rojos* were going to spoil it all for Papa.

Well, they wouldn't. Not if she could help it.

Camila glanced at the big man next to her in the driving seat. His tiny eyes were fixed on the road ahead. Yes, he was a giant, but he was also a stupid giant. That much was clear to her. *Very* stupid.

And she was *la chica inteligente...*

Yurichenko put down the device he was working on and looked up as Gordiovski came into the fishing vessel's cabin, the Spanish *señorita* at his side. Even with her dishevelled hair and tear-streaked face, she was a pretty little thing, no doubt about that. If he were her daddy, he certainly wouldn't want anything to happen to her.

Yurichenko felt a stab of emotion as he thought of his own daughter, Irina. It was so long since he'd seen her. She would be just a little older than this girl, almost fifteen. A young adult. He wondered how she was, how she was coping. It broke his heart to think of it.

He swallowed, gathered himself as Camila stared at him, her dark eyes full of hatred. 'Hola, *señorita*,' he said. 'Be good, and all will be well.' To Gordiovski he said, 'Sit her down. Give her something to eat and drink.'

Gordiovski grunted and pulled the girl by the arm. She tore herself away and glared at him, arms at her side, fists bunched, chin jutting aggressively. Gordiovski laughed. 'A spirited one.' He lunged, caught her by the neck. 'Sit down!'

Camila yelped but did as she was told.

'*Easy*,' Yurichenko warned. 'No damage, all right? I don't want to see a mark on her.'

'Of course, Alek.'

Yurichenko glared.

Gordiovski gave him a look, the disdainful, disrespectful look he'd received too many times on this trip. 'Yes, *Kapitan*.'

Yurichenko started the engine, checked his bearings. The boat chugged and vibrated beneath him. When he was satisfied, he went out and untied the moorings. Dawn was breaking and people would soon be up and about.

Time they weren't here.

Camila sat compliantly in the cabin. She was used to the movement of the boat, the tides, the deep waters around this, her own coastline. When the man *Gordy* called the *Kapitan* onto the deck to look at something, she went straight to the shelf next to the cabin controls where the man had been fiddling with something; a small, square box – like a radio.

Camila glanced outside to make sure no one was watching, and prised the little box open. It was filled with small wires and tiny parts. She felt sure it was something *los Rojos* would use against her Papa. Well, she'd soon see to that.

The internal parts were small, but her fingers were slim and dainty. Camila carefully extracted a miniscule brown board with tiny blobs of silver connecting even smaller pieces together, and put it in her pocket. She closed the lid, replaced the box where she'd found it and sat down just as the *Kapitan* and the big man came back into the cabin. She hoped she'd spoiled the thing for them, whatever it was.

Camila sat quietly and carefully watched everything the men were doing to see what else they might be up to. Whatever she could damage or disrupt for them, she would do it without hesitation. These were bad men.

And she was *la chica inteligente...*

11

The reek of fish made Kyle's stomach turn. When Francisco cast off and the boat began to rise and fall in the swell he took a breath and went to the railing above the hold, gripped it until his knuckles whitened.

'Keep your eyes on the horizon. It helps.' Bates advised.

'I'd forgotten how much I hate boats,' he said. 'Seawater in general, in fact.'

'Sorry, no alternative. At least it'll take your mind off the headaches.'

'Thanks for that.'

She stood next to him as they watched the harbour recede into the distance, the boat's wake carving white troughs in the deeper blue of the water. If he hadn't been feeling so rough it might even have been enjoyable.

Bates said, 'Sorry to have to tell you this, but we're going to have to disappear when we have sight of their rendezvous vessel.'

'I'd figured that out.'

'Only be for a short while, until we draw alongside. They'll be busy. And they know Francisco's boat.'

'You mean we'll have to go below, don't you?'

She nodded. 'You can hold your breath.'

'Funny.'

Seagulls followed them, wheeling and squawking, as Francisco gunned the engine and the little boat sped out into deeper waters.

'No fish for you guys, today,' Bates turned her face to the sky.

Kyle clung to the rail. 'I'm hoping you've had time to refine your plans a little?'

'Let's just say they're still fluid.'

'And don't talk about fish.'

'Noted.' She glanced sideways at him and grinned. She took a gulp of sea air. 'I love being out here. Makes you feel alive.'

Kyle kept his thoughts to himself.

A short while later, Francisco called from the cabin door. *'El barco!'*

'That's our cue, Kyle.'

Bates led the way into the hold, treading carefully on the damp wooden ladder. She waited for Kyle to descend and, once he'd reached floor level, she closed the hatch above them. Kyle had time to briefly admire her athletically-toned body before the daylight was shut out. The heat and smell were suddenly overpowering.

'Not sure I can cope with this.'

'Just ten minutes or so. Breathe through your mouth.'

He found a crate and sat down. 'You're aware that I have no experience of submersibles?'

'Yep. Nor me, for that matter.'

He heard her scrabbling around, searching for somewhere to sit. 'This warhead. It's a real threat? We're not putting our necks on the line for some bog-standard explosive device?'

'All the intelligence points to it being biological, I'm afraid.'

'Uh huh. And SIS are never wrong.'

'Not in this case, Kyle. These guys are for real. They've been on the case for a while. If it weren't for Russian intelligence, we'd still be in the dark.'

Kyle peered through the gloom. 'Funny, that.'

'You know what I mean.'

'And you really think they're crazy enough to detonate it? Here? On the Spanish coast?'

'I do, yes. And they'll make sure it's the Americans who get the blame.'

They felt the boat slowing as Francisco cut the engine, and the vessels pitching grew more pronounced. Kyle clenched his buttocks and imagined himself somewhere else.

Bates went on. 'That's why we can't allow them to salvage. It stays down there, where it can't do any harm.'

'Provided it doesn't go off.'

'Unlikely – not at that depth, and not without the correct priming. And if we make sure it tips into that fissure, it's game over. They'll never get it out.'

There was a jerk and the boat rocked, almost unseating him. 'What was that?'

'Anchor.' Bates was on her feet. 'Francisco's a little heavy-handed.'

'So what now?'

'Wait until Francisco's boarded. They'll get busy, then we join the party.'

Kyle let out a resigned sigh, inhaled deeply, then realised his mistake as the odour of countless dead fish assailed his nostrils. Gagging, he went to a corner and bent double, retching.

'I'll open the hatch as soon as I think it's safe.'

Kyle spat, grunted.

'Come on, Kyle. It's only fish.'

He heaved again, took another breath, straightened up.

More noises from the deck. Bates threw him a grim look. Bates whispered hoarsely, 'I need you in Giza mode, Kyle. Preferably soon,' she hissed.

'I'll bear that in mind.' Desperate for fresh air, he felt his way to the steps, climbed up the slimy slats and put his ear to the hatch. Ignoring Bates' whispered warning, he groped for the hatch release.

It sprang open surprisingly easily and a slit of daylight illuminated their prison. He took a gulp of salt-laden air, scanned left to right. To the left, all he could see was the bulk of a larger ship's exterior – rusted rivets and peeling paintwork – and the sound of gentle scraping and nudging as the two vessels rubbed against their tyre fenders. From much higher above, voices were engaged in staccato conversation. Not Spanish.

Russian.

He gently closed the hatch and made his way down. 'It's big, whatever it is. Not a fishing boat, that's for sure.'

'It's an RVK-1148 – a salvage support vessel. Two submersible's on board, one piloted, one robotic.'

'How do you know that?'

'Briefings.'

A pause as Kyle digested this. 'You're full of surprises, Bates.'

'I like to be informed. I like to know what I'm getting myself into.'

'If only I'd had the same opportunity—'

'I've already apologised for that.'

'I don't recall accepting your apology, though.'

'I'm a patient woman.'

Bates nimbly ascended to the hatch and opened it a crack. After a moment she opened it wider and motioned to Kyle. 'All clear.'

Crouched low on the deck, she beckoned him to join her as

he emerged into the sunlight. The contrast between the hold and the dazzling Spanish morning was profound. He blinked, took a grateful gulp of clean sea air.

Bates was scanning the deck above. 'Let's hope Francisco keeps his cool.'

'Would you?'

'I'd find it hard. But he knows they'll carry out their threat if he kicks off.'

'He's Spanish, though.' Kyle's eyes were beginning to adjust to the brightness. He blinked again.

'Hot-blooded?' Bates frowned. 'Maybe, but he's not stupid.'

Kyle grabbed the railing as the boat lurched to port and back again, bumping against the fenders.

'Bit rougher than usual today.' Bates scanned the sky. 'Could be a storm on the way.'

'Meteorologist, too? Is there no end to your—'

'*Shh!*' Bates' finger went to her lips.

Above them, two deckhands had appeared by the salvage vessel's railing, high above them and to the right. They leaned over, smoking and chatting. The cabin afforded them scant cover. If one of the sailors glanced down, he'd see them straight away.

'Follow me.'

Maintaining her crouching posture, Bates crept to the edge of the deck, climbed up to the railing and placed her right foot in a tyre well. She reached up, grabbed a railing post and hoisted herself onto the RVK-1148's deck.

Kyle watched with a combination of admiration and alarm. She'd kept herself fit while she was inside, and then some – or maybe SIS had inducted her with a rigorous physical training regime before deploying her. She gestured for him to follow.

He waited until the two men seemed more absorbed in

their conversation and made a run for the tyre. He got his foot inside and scrabbled for the railing post, but slipped as the larger vessel pitched away from him and almost lost his grip. A moment of lurching panic followed until a firm hand closed around his wrist, steadied him, and hauled him up onto the Russian deck.

'Thanks,' he whispered. Bates grinned and turned away to scan the deck.

They were crouched in the shadow of a large submersible, secured to the deck in a kind of iron cradle. The underwater vessel itself was stubby, mottled grey in colour, with a tall conning tower and some kind of clamping device affixed to its nose.

Bates ran her hand over its surface and made appreciative noises. 'Nice. More advanced than anything the US have, by the look of it – or ourselves for that matter. The Yanks used a much smaller sub.'

'No surprises there. The Russians have been busy.' Kyle was keeping an eye on the matelots, but just as he was about to suggest a safer vantage point, they threw their cigarette butts into the sea and disappeared into the ship's interior.

'OK,' Bates tapped the side of the submersible. 'First things first. Let's get you inside.'

'Now?'

'It makes sense. They'll want to deploy it sooner rather than later. You won't have long to wait.'

Bates was already moving around the body of the submersible, searching for the entry point. Towards the rear, there was a ladder affixed to the hull. High above, the outline of a hatch was just visible. She turned to him and raised her eyebrows.

Kyle narrowed his eyes. 'You sure about this?'

'You get the glory. I'll get the girl.'

'Wrong.' He shook his head. 'The hero usually gets the

girl.'

'Ha ha.'

'Seriously, Bates, I have no clue how to do this.'

She shrugged. 'Improvise, Kyle. That's what you're good at. Here, take this.' She pressed a small automatic into his hand. 'Be careful where you point it down there. You don't want a hole in the hull – it's pretty thick but I wouldn't put it to the test.'

He zipped the pistol into his pocket. 'What about ...' He struggled to remember the word for the condition she'd mentioned earlier. 'The depressurising thing?'

'The bends? The sub is pressurised to sea level pressure all the way. You'll be fine – while you're inside, of course. And I'll take care of Francisco and Camila, don't worry.'

'Perish the thought.' He placed one foot on the ladder and climbed quickly to the conning tower. The hatch was a circle of plated steel. He grabbed the handle and pulled. It opened easily on well-lubricated bearings. No time to hang around – anyone casting an idle glance from the rear of the bridge would be sure to spot him. He slipped through the aperture, reached up and closed the hatch. A rubber-runged ladder set into the wall of a dark, narrow tube at his feet pointed the way.

I must be completely nuts...

He turned and stepped gingerly onto the first rung.

12

The interior of the submersible was cramped and stuffy. A feeling of claustrophobia made Kyle shiver as he scanned left right and centre for a bolt hole large enough to accommodate his six foot plus frame. No easy task. He was momentarily grateful for the low diffused lighting that helped him find his way without tripping and injuring himself, but less than a second later his knee came into contact with unyielding metalwork and he cursed under his breath.

The hatch opened and a shaft of daylight spilled into the interior. Kyle froze. Voices, the shuffle of descending feet.

Anywhere will do…

He squeezed beneath a rack of shelving that supported a battery of complex electronics – communication or navigation equipment, he had no idea, but it was at the rear of the submersible, in the shadows and out of the way of the main control area. It would suffice.

Kyle wondered how many bodies the submersible could accommodate at any one time. Was the oxygen supply limited? Would there be some indication that levels were running suspiciously lower than expected, which might prompt the crew to conduct a search for stowaways? And how many men would the crew comprise anyway? He didn't fancy the odds of an uneven fight against two, maybe three angry Russians in such a confined space.

It seemed some of his fears were unfounded, at least; only one pair of feet arrived at the foot of the ladder, clad in tough rubber boots with cuffs of thick, woollen socks rolled down over the top. Their owner shouted a command and the hum of external hydraulics preceded a series of jerky movements signalling that the sub was being lifted from the deck.

Kyle breathed again. One on one were reasonable odds, and he had all the advantage of surprise. All he needed to do was judge the right moment to reveal himself and then force the pilot to tip the warhead over the edge of the fissure Bates had described. The practicalities of the procedure were not his problem; the pilot would know what to do, and the pilot would also find a gun pointing at him. Kyle checked his pocket for the reassuring contours of the automatic. He had a momentary flash of concern over what might ensue when they returned to the surface, but pushed the thought aside; the surface was Bates' department.

The pilot was busy at the controls, headphones clamped to his ears, pressing buttons, setting gauges, responding to some unheard set of instructions with grunts of affirmation. From his vantage point Kyle could see the single observational porthole, set into the sub's thick hull like the baleful eye of an octopus. As he watched, it turned a greeny-blue colour. He became aware of an airless, floating sensation. Motors hummed. Kyle held tightly to the shelving as the pilot pointed the submersible nose-down and they sank serenely towards the sea bed.

Time passed. There was little sensation of movement, only a curious weightlessness which was not together unpleasant. How long should he wait? Even if he'd been able to hear the communication between the pilot and the surface vessel, he would have been none the wiser. Perhaps the close manoeuvring of the vessel into position near the warhead would be indication enough that it was time for him to step in. He kept his eye on the porthole, not that it revealed a great deal except the murky, darkening hue of the water and the occasional curious marine creature.

He started as the pilot's voice yelled something unintelligible. The outburst was followed by a fusillade of banging as the Russian thumped the panelling. Something untoward had occurred. Kyle risked a look. The man had risen from his cramped position and moved to the porthole, clenching and unclenching his fists, muttering under his breath. Kyle looked past him and saw something grey floating past the porthole, trailing tendrils of what looked like rope or cord.

Still cursing, the pilot pressed his face to the glass and then returned to the pilot's station. Kyle was puzzled, and listened hard for clues as the conversation with the surface vessel resumed.

One word jumped out.

It sounded like *parachute*.

Of course. The bombs would have been designed to parachute down and detonate just before contact with the ground. This one clearly still had its canopy attached, despite its years on the sea bed.

That would make recovery a messy business. They'd need to sever the chute from the bomb casing, or it would hinder their ascent; parachutes worked just as well in water as they did in the air.

No sooner had the thought occurred to him than the submersible yawed violently and came to a shuddering stop. Kyle held onto the shelving as the sub began to spin slowly on its axis. A fresh bout of cursing from the direction of the pilot station confirmed that things were not going to plan. Another heated exchange with the surface as the sub continued its erratic revolutions also confirmed Kyle's fears; somehow, they had become entangled in the chute.

He felt himself grow cold as he considered the implications. Unless the sub could be freed, both he and the pilot were trapped down here until the air ran out.

The pilot removed his headphones, leaned back and rested his head on the back of his chair.

Thinking time.

In this situation, Kyle reasoned, two heads were preferable. He and the pilot were in this together, with a common interest, it had to be assumed, of staying alive. The fate of the warhead might prove to be a source of disagreement at some future point, but for now...

He rolled out from beneath the shelving and got stiffly to his feet. There wasn't much headroom and he moved cautiously forward in the same crouching manner he'd watched the pilot employ a few minutes before.

In the absence of any better way to introduce himself, he simply said: 'I'm hoping you speak English better than I speak Russian.'

The man shot out of his bucket seat and turned to face Kyle.

He was fast. *Very* fast.

They eyed each other. The man facing Kyle was a little older, maybe in his early forties, but with scarcely an ounce of fat. He was lean, muscle-toned, and dressed in a close-fitting oilskin jacket, dark trousers and the boots Kyle had seen descend the ladder. The Russian's hair was cropped, greying at the temples. The jaw was strong, well-defined, and blue with half a day's stubble.

'Who the hell are *you*?'

Kyle held up his empty hands, palms out. 'Ah, good. No language barrier.'

The man's eyes narrowed. '*Gavno...* You are the British

man – the replacement.'

'It's complicated.' Kyle stayed quite still. He had to show this man he meant him no harm.

'That idiot, Gordiovski,' the man muttered.

'Your colleague, the big chap? We've met. Not too friendly.'

'He is ... careless.' The man's hands were still working, fists clenching, unclenching.

Kyle held out his hand. 'Cameron Kyle. I think we need to work together.' He waited for the Russian to remember their joint predicament.

'Alek Yurichenko.' The hand was presented cautiously, but the grip was firm enough.

'We're entangled, correct?' Kyle pointed to the porthole where drifting strands of parachute cord were still visible.

'Da.'

I'm guessing you'll need someone to assist. While you cut the chute cords.'

Yurichenko said nothing. He was still weighing his options.

The Russian's headset crackled, a tinny voice repeating prompts for acknowledgment. Yurichenko wet his lips, glanced at the communication device, then back to Kyle.

'I do not need your help.'

Kyle reluctantly took out the automatic. 'I'm sorry, but I must take charge at this point.'

Yurichenko seemed unfazed by the sight of the pistol. He smiled thinly. 'You don't look like a naval man,' he said. 'You don't know how to navigate. You don't have any idea what to do.'

'I can assist you. But I'm afraid the warhead won't be coming back up with us.'

Yurichenko laughed, shook his head. He sat down and looked at Kyle with a mixture of amusement and resignation. After a short silence he nodded.

'You're right, it won't be.'

Now it was Kyle's turn to look discombobulated. 'I'm sorry?'

'You heard correctly.' Yurichenko nodded towards the headset. 'May I?'

'Go on. Slowly, please.'

With exaggerated deliberation, Yurichenko picked up the headset and disconnected the lead. 'Good. Now we have a private talk. So, please put the gun down, Mr Kyle. I think we both want the same thing.'

13

'Is that so?' Kyle kept the automatic pointed directly at the Russian's head. 'Explain.'

Yurichenko folded his arms. 'No time for the full life story, Mr Kyle; perhaps a short summary, though. If you would be kind enough to lower your pistol?'

Kyle checked the contours of the Russian's clothing. There was nowhere to conceal a weapon, and there was something about Yurichenko that engendered trust. He put the gun back in his pocket.

'All right, but I think we'll both be more comfortable when we've regained control of the sub, don't you?'

Yurichenko shrugged. 'I will use the robot to cut us free. If I steer her accurately it should not be a problem.'

The Russian seemed confident. Kyle recalled Bates mentioning that the support vessel had both manned and unmanned submersibles at its disposal, but hadn't realised that the former carried the latter. 'Fire away,' he said, 'I'm listening.'

'Very well. 'Yurichenko folded his arms. 'I, no doubt like yourself, Mr Kyle, have served my country for many years – from a very early age. This, you understand, I wanted for myself; it was not forced upon me. For me, the Motherland was everything; my upbringing pushed me inevitably in this direction. I joined the navy at sixteen. I worked hard, did well, joined the Northern Fleet, rose through the ranks to eventually captain the most powerful nuclear submarines. I have sailed beneath the Arctic ice caps, seen action in many campaigns, been awarded the Order of the Red Banner for my dedication to service.'

Yurichenko paused, and Kyle allowed him a moment to gather his thoughts. Eventually the Russian gave a long sigh and continued.

'An unfortunate… no, a *bad* situation arose. I was made a …' Yurichenko clicked his fingers as he searched for the word. 'A *scapegoat*, yes?' He spread his hands, 'I was not to blame for the situation, but suspicion fell upon me. Our secret service are nothing if not persistent, Mr Kyle. In summary, I lost my captaincy, and subsequently also my wife Nadya, who was consumed by shame at my supposed misconduct. All lies' He paused, his lips compressed. '*All* lies. She took my daughter, and left me. But then, and even worse, Nadya was imprisoned along with my daughter for an apparent contravention of state policy. This was an insane, unwarranted accusation. Nevertheless, they are both still serving time in a labour camp. Since then, I have enjoyed the constant attention of the KGB, and one dogsbody assignment after another. This being the latest and, in my opinion, the most foolhardy.'

Kyle nodded again. 'I see. I'm sorry for what you've suffered.' The strangeness of the situation had disarmed him; a senior Russian naval officer confessing a disastrous falling out with his seniors? Strange or not, it seemed as though he'd found an unexpected ally.

He needed to be sure, though. 'The warhead. Am I to understand that you have alternative plans to those of your seniors?'

Yurichenko shot him a bitter smile. 'I do not care about the warhead. I care even less to arm and deploy it in an innocent country.'

'Good to hear, but I'm assuming Ygor upstairs thinks differently?'

'Ygor?' Yurichenko looked nonplussed for a moment, but then laughed. 'Ah, Gordiovski.' He became serious again. 'Gordiovski will complete the task he has been set, unless he is stopped.' A pause. 'However, at this point, I would like to put on record that I did not send him to kill you, Mr Kyle. His task was to neutralise any threat to the operation, and as I understood it, this sprang primarily from the agent in situ, Miss Bates.'

'Bates is a friend of mine.'

Yurichenko shrugged apologetically. 'You understand I have to follow through, otherwise Gordiovski becomes suspicious of my true motives. But I assume that, like yourself, Miss Bates is still alive?'

Kyle confirmed this with a nod.

'But this is splendid, no? Yurichenko smiled, spread his hands. 'Here we have a unique situation, an opportunity to work together.'

'Gordiovski can't be allowed to recover the warhead,' Kyle said. 'As you say, the Spanish are blameless. They've already suffered enough over the American incident. A biological weapon would wreak havoc on this coast. Thousands of innocents would die.'

'The Spanish?' Yurichenko raised his thick eyebrows. 'Who said anything about the Spanish? Our brief is to deploy the warhead over London.'

14

Kyle took a moment. 'Did I hear that correctly?' His voice was flat in the pressurised cabin, his mouth dry.

Yurichenko returned an even, unflinching look.

'And how exactly is that to be implemented?'

Yurichenko paused for a moment, collecting his thoughts. 'The blame is to be attached to a minor terrorist organisation. Our intelligence service is already preparing disinformation concerning the possible interest of this group in the lost bioweapon. Much emphasis is to be made of the origins of the weapon, the fact that it remains the responsibility of the US. Their failure to recover it – or even to admit its existence – will ensure that they take the brunt of the fallout – excuse me for the bad pun – after the event.'

'An anthrax attack. On London. You can't be serious.'

'On the contrary, Mr Kyle. My superiors are deadly serious.'

'It will kill *thousands*. Maybe more—'

'Undoubtedly, but—' Yurichenko made a dismissive gesture. 'You and I, we will ensure that it does not happen.' He extended his hand again. 'Are we in agreement, Mr Kyle?'

Kyle held his gaze, then shook the proffered hand. 'But where will this leave you, *Kapitan* Yurichenko?'

Yurichenko smiled, a sad, reflective movement of his lips. 'You have an expression, I think? Between a boulder and … ah, I forget…'

'A rock and a hard place?' Kyle suggested.

'*Da*. Precisely.' Yurichenko reprised his smile. 'But enough of me. Now we have reached an understanding, we should address our predicament.'

'The remote submersible?'

'Yes.'

'And I can't help?'

'You can observe. And as you are from a Christian country, I think you can also pray.'

Kyle's mouth, previously dry, now felt like sandpaper. 'Not many Christians left in the UK, but I take your point. How deep are we?'

Yurichenko consulted one of the many dials on the pilot control panel. 'Deep enough.'

'And your remote sub; how does it work?'

'The machine is cable-controlled. It is fundamentally a lightweight frame with ballast tanks. We have two cameras, a grappling device and a cutter. It is attached beneath us and controllable either from here or from our support ship.'

'You'd better update Gordiovski. He'll be suspicious of a lengthy comms silence.'

Yurichenko nodded, reattached the lead from the headphones. He spoke rapidly in Russian, listened, spoke again then removed the headset. 'I have told him that we must cut ourselves free. He is pleased that we have located the warhead so quickly – it took the Americans a very long time to find the last one.'

'Francisco was of great value to you.'

A nod.

'I hope you will treat his family accordingly.'

'For myself, da. I cannot speak for Gordiovski.'

'Good to know he's concerned for the safety of his *Kapitan*.'

'Hah! Gordy cares only about success.'

Kyle watched the Russian selecting various options on the sub's comprehensive dashboard, adjusting knobs and switches, checking dials and glancing every so often at a small TV monitor, until eventually he gave a grunt of satisfaction and sat back in the pilot's seat.

'Good. I think everything is in place. I must first disengage the remote submersible.'

'Let's hope we're not completely caught up in the chute.'

'We will soon see.' Yurichenko leaned forward and slowly moved a rubber-coated joystick from its neutral position to the first in a series of narrow slots annotated with some unreadable Russian abbreviation. Kyle paid close attention. He was uncomfortably aware that his life was completely in the Russian's hands. Guiltily, he remembered that Bates was also in a perilous situation, alone, on board a Russian ship with no backup.

He pushed that thought from his mind. What was happening now was critical – if Yurichenko failed to disentangle them, they were in big trouble and he would be in no position to support Bates in her efforts to free both Francisco and his daughter from their captors. The positives – that they had found the warhead and that Yurichenko was his unlikely ally – offered little comfort in the face of the horrific implications of the Russian intention to deploy the bomb over London. Whatever happened in the immediate future, though, the warhead was not going to be recovered – not if he had anything to do with it.

Yurichenko was communicating with the surface vessel in short, staccato phrases as he guided the remote submersible to its destination. Kyle was glued to the small screen. It was hard to make out anything with any clarity, but Kyle trusted that the Russian's experience would be enough to guide the auxiliary craft in a circle of reconnaissance to establish their best approach.

'There.'

Kyle followed the Russian's prompt. On the screen the camera picked out a cylindrical object, half-buried in silt on the seabed. From the rear of the canister, grey ribbons of parachute cord shimmied and danced in the deep currents.

Yurichenko manoeuvred the joystick and their own submersible swam into view. Above them, the chute canopy wafted like a breeze-blown beach umbrella, the tendrils of thick cord loosely wrapped around one of the extended manipulator arms.

'Not a bad problem,' Yurichenko muttered under his breath. He moved the joystick again, eased it to the right, reached forward and gripped a smaller but similar control stick on an adjacent control panel. He spoke into the headset microphone. The earphones crackled as the surface vessel responded.

Kyle held his breath as the distance closed.

'I have to be close, so there is a risk that the remote could also be caught.'

Kyle wasn't sure whether the Russian was addressing him or thinking aloud. They were both glued to the screen as the remote's long cutter arm extended towards the cord.

Suddenly a silvery brown object caught the camera's eye and in the next second it had obscured their view altogether. Yurichenko swore and wiggled the joystick. As the Russian held the submersible's position, Kyle saw what had caused the blackout; a large grouper fish was swimming languidly around their vessel, as though conducting an inspection.

'Again,' Yurichenko muttered.

Their sub came back into view as the grouper drifted away, losing interest in the strange object hovering in its domain. The Russian zoomed in on a single cord, the cause of their entrapment. Yurichenko flicked a switch and a second spotlight lit up the bows of their submersible. The grabber claw was clearly visible, and around it the loosely encircled chute cord.

Once again the remote sub moved in closer, and closer still until Yurichenko cut the power, reached forward and selected a toggle switch from the panel of instruments in front of him. It was an impressively skilful manoeuvre; as the remote drifted powerless at their bow, Yurichenko extended the cutter arm and deftly severed the cord with a single snap of the shear-like cutters.

There was a jerk as the submersible lurched upwards. Yurichenko immediately gunned the engines and piloted them away from the waving chute. Suspended in the void below them, the remote's twin mercury vapour spotlights cut parallel beams of light through the murky water like the baleful eyes of some deepwater demon.

Yurichenko piloted the small sub to the seabed, allowed it to hover beside the half-buried cylinder, and then drew a relieved breath. 'More light, I think.'

'Excellent work, *Kapitan* Yurichenko.' Kyle was impressed. The Russian was an expert in every sense of the word. He squinted through the porthole as the remote's spotlights picked out a shadowy gash in the seabed only a few metres from the cylindrical shape of the warhead – the crevasse. It shouldn't prove too difficult to nudge it over the edge; the manoeuvre would surely be more straightforward than the one they had just undertaken.

Yurichenko was speaking to the surface vessel in short, sharp sentences that sounded to Kyle like a series of instructions and confirmations.

'What are you telling them?' Kyle leaned in closer, as if that would somehow help him to understand the rapid-fire Russian exchange.

Yurichenko finished his conversation and removed the headset.

'I am sorry to say that Gordiovski has found your friend.' The Russian lifted his hand and rubbed his ear, as though the headset had irritated the skin.

'My—?'

Kyle saw it coming but was too close to the Russian to take evasive action. The ear rubbing had been designed to give the blow its most efficient trajectory. Yurichenko's elbow smashed into his temple and the lights went out as though someone had thrown a switch.

15

Kyle floated slowly upward into semi-consciousness as the submersible broke the surface and began to bob impatiently in the choppy water. Daylight filtered into the sub's interior through the porthole, a shaft of sunlight that lanced Kyle's half-open eyes like a gimlet. He couldn't move his hands; they were trussed securely, as were his legs. Yurichenko had bundled him out of the way on the floor; he was resting near his original hiding place.

Immobility, however, wasn't Kyle's primary concern. He'd taken a hard blow to the head and his first, most worrying thought was that the bullet fragment might have been dislodged. The severity of his pain suggested as much, but right now there wasn't a great deal he could do about it.

The hatch opened, voices calling in from above. The tone was buoyant, congratulatory. Kyle cursed his own stupidity. He'd let his guard down, trusted a Russian naval officer, swallowed his story hook, line and sinker. Yurichenko had never intended to dispose of the warhead. He was on track with Moscow's mission. Kyle had to hand it to the Russian; Yurichenko had disarmed him with a sob story, turned a bad situation into an advantageous one with a persuasive biography and a promise of cooperation. Kyle groaned.

Idiot, Kyle. Idiot...

Worse still, they'd found Bates. He shivered as he considered the possibility they'd killed her out of hand. She was, after all, an MI6 agent. Those were the rules of the game; you make a mistake, you pay for it.

More shouting, followed by the clunk of machinery, the whirring of the support vessel's winch. The moment of separation from the water was a sucking, swaying lurch that made his stomach turn. Something banging against the hull, the winch motor rising to a crescendo, a further jarring jolt as the submersible was reunited with its cradle. Footsteps descended. A pair of boots at eye level. The foot swung back, kicked him hard in the ribs. Pain sliced through his torso, eclipsing the pain in his head. 'OK, Mr Spy. Time to meet the crew.'

Yurichenko; no longer the genial brother-in-arms, now showing his true colours.

Hands reached for him, dragged him to his knees, his feet. His feet were untied. Someone grabbed his hair, pulled his head back. 'Hey Alek, the Brits are recruiting hippies now, eh?' A vicious slap to his cheek.

Laughter.

Another blow, this time to his shoulders. Someone pushed him so hard that he stumbled at the base of the ladder, lost his footing, cracked his head on the floor. His skull was on fire. He felt himself lifted, pushed up the rubber rungs into the daylight.

'He is security services virgin, I think Alek. No good for the spooks.'

Another voice. 'Maybe that's why they sent him, eh? No other use for him.'

Through aching eyes Kyle tracked his progress through the ship's interior, marking corridors, labels, any defining features, committing them to memory. They went down one level, two. Another ladder, a short, iron staircase. A steel hatch. The leading man unlocked it and rough hands shoved him forward. The hatch slammed behind him.

The ship's engines throbbed like the heartbeat of some prehistoric serpent. The darkness was absolute. He found a wall and slid to his haunches, felt blood trickle down his face into the corner of his mouth, a sour, metallic taste.

Something shuffled nearby, the movement of some living thing. He recoiled, thinking of rats, or worse. Then a familiar voice:

'Kyle? Is that you?'

16

'Bates. Good to hear you.'

A pause. 'I didn't know you cared.'

'Let's not get ahead of ourselves.' Kyle winced at the effort of speech.

'You're hurt.'

'It's only a problem if I breathe.'

'That does actually sound like a problem. What happened? … In your own time.'

Kyle told her, pausing occasionally to take small sips of air.

When he finished there was a brief silence. Eventually Bates said, 'So what happened to Giza mode?'

'Never showed.'

'Right.' No mistaking the disappointment in the single syllable.

'Must have been a one-off.' Kyle rested his head on the bulkhead.

'I could remind you about Wales. Or maybe you just weren't mad enough at the thought of Spain being poisoned? And don't forget your medic's assessment – you're a risk-taking, borderline psychopath now, remember?'

Should he mention London? Not yet. 'I let my guard down. I was stupid.'

'Not arguing with that.'

'Thanks.'

'And you're still not mad enough?'

'Mad enough, but slightly incapacitated.'

'So, presented with an opportunity to get even, you'd decline?'

Kyle clenched his teeth. 'Probably not, actually.'

'Good. That's all I wanted to know. I mean, the Giza guys didn't get close, did they?'

'Technically, one actually did.'

'And what happened to him?'

'Crushed under the coach.'

'There you go. I humbly submit that you have reasons to be even madder this time around.'

'Point taken.'

'Good. Let's talk about the warhead. They have it, I assume.'

'Yes.'

'And we're not doing any good stuck in here.'

Kyle grunted. It hurt less than forming a word. He heard her shuffle across the floor and, a moment later, the arhythmic pounding of her feet on the metalwork of the hatch.

She stopped momentarily. 'Could do with some help.'

Kyle considered the request. Every movement drove a spike of pain through his temple, but nevertheless he half-crawled, half-shuffled on his backside until he was next to her. Then he closed his eyes, willed himself to enter some Zen-like state where he could separate his mind from the pain and walk away. He positioned his feet next to Bates and went for it.

The noise was cacophonous. They heard an angry voice followed by a reciprocal bang on the outside of the hatch. Easy to interpret: *Shut up.*

They rested for a few seconds.

'When it opens?'

'Go for the shins, hard as you can.'

'Might be more than one of them.'

'That's one each.'

'You can't handle both?'

'Just kick the door, Kyle.'

Kyle made himself do what Bates asked. His head pulsed with the effort.

He paused for breath.

'Come *on*, Kyle.'

'Wait. It's gone quiet.'

They both strained to hear.

Nothing.

Bates drew back her leg to start kicking again but Kyle grabbed her arm. '*Wait.*'

A metallic scraping. Kyle put his ear to the hatch.

A crack of light. The hatch door banged against his legs. They shuffled back together as it swung fully open. Bates was next to him, coiled like a spring, ready to inflict damage.

A silhouette.

Bates lashed out but Kyle caught her leg and held it fast.

'Get *off* me, Kyle!' She tried to free herself.

Kyle held on.

A slight figure stepped forward, tentatively ... fearfully.

Kyle felt Bates go limp.

'*Hola.*' Camila stepped into the light in the companionway outside the hatch. 'I am so happy I found you.'

17

The light was dim, but not so dim that they couldn't see the prone figure of a Russian naval subaltern curled up on the floor like a sleeping baby.

Camila hunkered down and whispered hoarsely in Bates' ear. She then produced a knife and began to saw through the cord around Bates' wrists. Kyle watched the girl, fascinated. She seemed calm, almost casual. Bates shot him a warning glance. *No questions yet, OK?*

Kyle turned his attention to the corridor. He could see some way along it, but it turned to the right after thirty feet or so. He remembered a staircase, and then the corner shortly after; if someone approached they'd have little warning. He squinted at the Russian sailor. Out cold. But what was that next to him on the floor? He focused on the object. A test-tube? A vial of some sort? No ... a syringe.

Bates was at his side, rubbing her wrists. 'Insulin. Like I said, she's a smart kid. Here–' She brandished the knife. 'Give me your hands.'

She rapidly freed him and he got to his haunches, more slowly to his feet. His temple pounded like a bass drum. He leaned on the metal wall for support.

Bates turned her attention back to Camila. '*Ingles, por favor,*

Camila.' She nodded in Kyle's direction. The girl looked at him with huge, brown eyes. Kyle could see they were red and tear-streaked.

'OK,' she said.

'Where is your father, Camila?' Kyle spoke in low tones, for the girl's sake and because he didn't want his voice to echo along the corridor.

'They don't need him,' she replied, the last word a half-sob. 'He has done his job. I think they will do something bad.' She gazed imploringly at him.

Kyle took her hand. 'No they won't. We're going to find him, aren't we, Bates?'

Bates nodded, forced a smile. 'We absolutely are. Camila, you've been very brave. How did you get away? How did you find us?'

'I watched the man when they put me in a room on my own. He put numbers and the door opens.'

'Two-way keypad,' Kyle said.

'When it is quiet again, I click the numbers and the door opens.' Camila moistened her lips. Her hair was tangled and she brushed a stray wisp from her cheek, where the tear tracks stood out against the brown of her flawless skin. 'Before they leave me I hear the big man say where you will be. He said *dek 2, cuarto de servicio del motor.*'

'Engine utility room.' Bates shook her head in admiration.

'I follow the *señales,*' she went on. 'And I remember my *jeringuilla.* Papa says it is dangerous for *no diabéticos.* The man —' she pointed to the prone sailor, 'he comes to me, and I stick him, like *this.*' She made a sudden jabbing motion with her hand. 'He is angry, he hurts me.' She held up the evidence, a widening purple bruise on her forearm. 'And then he falls.' She shrugged.

'Never underestimate a child.' Kyle rested a hand on Camila's shoulder. 'Camila, it's going to be OK.' He made the universal OK sign with his thumb and middle finger and she flashed him a tight-lipped smile.

'I suggest a rapid exit.' Bates glanced along the passage. 'Can you walk, Kyle? How're the ribs?'

Kyle straightened, probed his ribcage and winced. 'Not great. My head is going to be a problem, though.'

'We'll find a first aid room. They'll have painkillers.'

'Industrial strength, I hope.' Kyle passed a hand across his damp forehead. He was used to tolerating headaches, a daily trial since he was shot, but Yurichenko had hurt him badly. Something had changed. He pictured the bullet fragment inside his cranium, a tiny but inevitable death sentence. Was it on the move? An image of his neurologist came to mind, his expression serious as he outlined the worst case scenario: *If you experience symptomatic changes, the rule of thumb is: straight to Casualty, understood? No messing around. There won't be time for that. I'll make sure your case notes are on hand for the staff. I'm sure they'll do their absolute best if ... should the worst come to the worst.*

'You remember where your papa is?' Bates took Camila's arm. The girl nodded. 'Kyle?'

'After you.'

'Here, take this.' Bates passed him Camila's knife, a double-edged, bone-handled blade with a wicked point. A sailor's knife. He wondered where Camila had found it. Didn't matter; he tucked it into his belt and led them to the foot of the staircase. As he placed a foot on the first rung he heard a metallic clatter from above.

'Down.'

They squeezed behind a bulkhead and waited, Bates with her arm around Camila. Footsteps grew louder, and Kyle positioned himself in the shadows behind the stairwell. Legs appeared, followed by the muscular body of a uniformed sailor.

Kyle broke cover and wrapped his arm around the man's neck, brought his free hand up to slide the knife into his chest. The Russian caught Kyle's wrist and held it, smashed his fist over his shoulder into Kyle's jaw. Kyle dropped the knife and slammed against the bulkhead as the Russian spun on his heels and charged him. He was squat, muscular and, by the look of him, more than used to a scrap.

Kyle dodged the fist that followed through and the man yelled as his punch met the unyielding steel of the bulkhead. Kyle went for the sailor's neck with a vicious karate chop, but again the man blocked him. It felt like he'd hit a brick wall. Pain shot up Kyle's arm like an electric current.

The sailor stood back, sizing him up. He raised his fists and grinned. He was enjoying the contest.

Just my luck ... a boxing champ...

Kyle raised his fists, dummied, and went for the knife, but the sailor had anticipated him. He aimed a well-placed kick that found Kyle's already damaged ribcage. The agony was so intense that for a split second Kyle was immobilised. His eyes registered the second kick on its way, the steel-capped boot swinging towards him. He grabbed the boot centimetres away from its target, and twisted hard. Something snapped with a satisfying *crack*, a bone or maybe a tendon.

The sailor screamed, teeth bared. Kyle kept hold of the leg and pushed. The Russian fell full-length onto his back. Kyle was on him in a second, the knife in his right hand. He buried it in the man's chest, and sat back on his haunches, panting.

'That's more like it,' Bates came forward.

Breathing heavily, Kyle got back on his feet. 'Thanks for your help, by the way.'

'I was protecting Camila.'

'No you bloody weren't. You wanted to see if I was mad enough.'

'Button it, Kyle. Let's get him out of sight.'

They dragged the dead sailor into the shadow of the stairwell. Bates found some offcuts of discarded sack cloth in the corner and covered him.

'His shirt – and hat.' Bates pointed.

'Really?'

'Yes. Extra seconds if we're challenged. Look, take his arm, that's right. Unbutton it – not like that … wait.' She brushed his efforts aside. 'Here. I'll do it.'

Sporting his new attire and supporting his ribcage with one hand while simultaneously attempting to cover the wide bloodstain on his borrowed shirt, Kyle led them cautiously up the metal stairs to a narrow corridor that apparently ran the length of the ship, regular sets of portholes filtering suffused light into the ship's interior. The clamour of hydraulics, rumbling of weighty machinery and sporadic, shouted instructions now competed with the throbbing of the ship's engines.

The door immediately ahead of them opened onto an empty deck. Kyle led them through; a quick check over the side revealed both fishing boats, Francisco's and the Russians', riding close at anchor,. In the centre of the Russian deck, the long, cylindrical shape of the recovered bomb was being gently lowered into a rectangular iron cradle. They watched the recovery vessel's jib swing slowly back to its place of origin aboard the RVK-1148. No one was looking in their direction; all attention was focused on the operation in progress.

Kyle gripped the railing, nodded towards the Russian fishing vessel. 'We need to be on board before it casts off.'

Bates was at his side, Camila's small hand firmly grasped in hers. 'A tricky proposition. And there's Francisco to consider,' she added quietly.

'There's a bomb to consider,' Kyle said. 'Priorities.'

Bates scowled as Camila looked up at her with a crestfallen expression. 'I know, Kyle. But we can't leave Francisco here.'

'You get the girl. I'm still chasing the glory, remember?'

'Ah, it's glory you seek, is it, Mr Kyle? A common ambition among you Brits, I believe?'

Kyle turned slowly. Yurichenko and the big guy were standing a few feet away, the latter pointing a wicked-looking AK-47 at Kyle's midriff.

'It was an in-joke, actually.'

'Ah – the British humour.' Yurichenko exchanged a knowing look with the big guy. 'What do you think, Gordy?'

The man addressed as Gordy shrugged. 'Not much for him to laugh about now, eh?'

Yurichenko went on. 'I'm afraid I must leave you in my colleague's care. I hope I did not inconvenience you too much, Mr Kyle?'

'With your captivating back story? Not at all – I'm a sucker for fiction.'

Yurichenko shook his head. 'I meant physically, Mr Kyle. I trust you are not in too much discomfort?'

'I'll cope.'

Yurichenko nodded to his colleague. 'Comrade Gordiovski will debrief you. Of course you understand that we cannot allow you to return to the mainland. You will remain on the ship and follow orders. I have preparations to make, so you must excuse me.'

'Let the girl and her father go.' Bates said. 'They've done nothing to hinder you.'

Yurichenko pondered this for a moment. 'That is not my decision,' he said eventually, and turned away. To Gordiovski he said, 'Do not delay, comrade. I shall expect you before nightfall.' He gave a stiff bow and disappeared below deck.

Gordiovski expertly frisked all three of them and confiscated the knife. 'Move.' He prompted them to walk ahead with a quick side-to-side movement of the AK-47's barrel.

Camila was in tears. As they descended into the ship's interior for the second time, they heard the Russian fishing boat's engines roar into life.

The bomb was headed towards land.

18

Following Gordiovski's barked orders, they were shepherded to a different area of the ship and eventually into a small room whose walls were covered with charts and maps, and with furniture consisting of a desk, three chairs and a filing cabinet. Some under-officer's quarters, maybe, Kyle, thought, or just an underused utility room.

'Sit.'

They sat.

Gordiovski checked the corridor, closed the door. Then he lowered the Kalashnikov. He looked Kyle full in the face. 'This may come as a surprise,' he began, 'but I want to help you.'

Kyle looked at Bates.

Gordiovski laid the automatic on the floor and straightened up. 'Yes. You heard me correctly. I want to help you. Moreover, I also wish to defect.'

There was silence. Camila glanced at Bates, unsure.

Gordiovski went on, his hands raised placatingly. 'No tricks. I will give you safe passage, but only in exchange for your help.'

'We'll just forget about the grenade at the hotel, then, shall we?' Kyle raised an eyebrow.

'Pfffh!' Gordiovski made a dismissive gesture. 'I removed half the charge. And gave you plenty of warning. It was never going to hurt you.'

'Then why?'

'A test. The *Kapitan's* desire, not mine. Were you ... *up to scratch*? Yes?'

Bates said, 'And the proprietress?'

'Collateral damage.' He shrugged. 'She has too much *slukhi*.' He mimed a talking mouth with his hand.

Kyle shared another look with Bates. Her expression was curious; confusion, maybe, but there was something else, something he couldn't put his finger on.

'Yurichenko means to see this through,' Gordiovski continued. 'But he needs me to arm the bomb. I will not do so; In fact, I will make certain it is disarmed. We will stop him.'

Bates was staring hard at the Russian in a way that was making Kyle uncomfortable, but he still couldn't figure out what was bothering him.

'And Francisco? What about him?' Bates' eyes widened and Kyle tensed; they only did that when she meant business.

'Yes, yes. He may go home. No use for him now or his little one.' Gordiovski shot a smile at Camila and she glared back at him.

Gordiovski was now in full flow. 'What did Yuri tell you, Mr Kyle? That he had made a mistake? That he was unfairly treated? That he was sidelined for further promotion? That his wife and child left him in order to hide from his disgrace, and then got themselves locked up?'

'Something along those lines.'

Gordiovski let out a grunt of satisfaction. 'Of course. Of course he did. But it is not so!' He slammed his huge fist into the wall, making Camila jump. 'That is *my* story, not his.'

'He lied. Yeah, no surprises there.' Kyle tried to breathe

gently. His ribs were sending lances of pain through his torso, his head responding with a pounding echo while his stomach rolled continually with the movement of the ship. The combination of pain and nausea was playing havoc with his ability to think – and clear thinking was precisely what was needed here.

He willed his brain into gear. Gordiovski's unexpected revelation had not only bought them time, but also the offer of escape and the chance to apprehend Yurichenko. He was curious about the Russian's *volte face* but now was not the time to launch into an in-depth interview with Gordiovski; that would be for later.

'Lies and more lies,' Bates nodded. 'Welcome to the world of espionage, Kyle.'

'Thanks. I guess I'll have to wait for the full induction course.' He stood up. 'By the way, why are we still here?'

Gordiovski nodded approvingly. 'Good. So we go. But please do exactly as I say. If you are questioned, remain silent. I will answer.' He reached for the door handle.

'There's just one small matter to consider before we leave,' Kyle said.

Gordiovski paused. 'Yes?'

'A casualty – one of the ship's personnel.'

'Dead, yes?'

'I'm afraid so – he started it, to be fair. Just to warn you, though. The crew might not be too happy about it.'

Gordiovski shrugged. 'Again, collateral damage. I will deal with it, if necessary.'

As it turned out, no one challenged them on their way to the disembarkation platform where Gordiovski gave terse instructions to an idling group of sailors. Kyle watched them jump to it. They didn't argue; not many would with someone of Gordiovski's size. The deckhands quickly untethered a ladder and positioned it with practised skill to allow access to

Francisco's restlessly bobbing fishing boat below.

A shout from above, and Camila tore herself from Bates' grip. 'Papa!'

Francisco was making his way towards them, flanked by two naval officers. The Spaniard looked none the worse for wear, although his expression left Kyle in little doubt about his feelings towards his captors. He joined them by the ladder and embraced his daughter as Bates descended gingerly to the fishing boat's deck, followed by Camila and Francisco. Then it was Kyle's turn, followed by Gordiovski, the big man moving down the rungs with surprising agility.

Kyle took a seat behind the cabin alongside Bates and Camila. Francisco headed inside and made preparations to cast off. The engine roared but before they made their departure Kyle caught a movement from above. Someone else was descending. No uniform, a dirty grey shirt, jeans, shapeless jacket. The man's head was shaved, and he had a small tattoo above his right ear. As he hit the deck Gordiovski noticed the direction of Kyle's attention.

'A little help, for tidying things.'

Kyle held the big man's gaze until a call from the support vessel above distracted him and he looked away. However, what he'd just read in Gordiovski's eyes didn't require any translation. It meant bad news for someone.

The fishing boat separated from the support ship like a chick disengaging from its mother. A line of Russian sailors watched them from the middle deck. They seemed ambivalent towards both the salvage operation and their departure. Just another job, another set of coordinates in the vastness of the ocean and the long years of their service to the Motherland.

Kyle steadied himself as the boat pitched on the swell, heading towards land. He felt the eyes of the newcomer on him, sizing him up. Some people you wouldn't turn your back on, and this guy was one of them.

A canvas-topped lorry was waiting for them at the harbour. Kyle leaned on the tail lift as Bates said her goodbyes to Francisco and Camila. The dusk was warm and the ground reassuringly solid under Kyle's feet. His ribs still throbbed but his headache was marginally better and the nausea had abated. Gordiovski and the tattooed guy wordlessly took the driver and passenger seat respectively. Bates was still on her haunches, speaking to Camila in a low voice. Kyle walked to the driver's window. 'Might be good to talk about this – before we attempt to round up your friend.'

Gordiovski scowled. 'The Kapitan is no friend of mine.'

'So you said. But it might be wise to have—'

'A plan? Yes. Here is plan. We shall meet him at the warehouse. You will stay in the vehicle. I and my comrade will deal with the Kapitan.' He fixed Kyle with another searching look and wiped his nose. 'There is a plane, a transporter. You will fly it to London. There you will take me to your superiors. I will speak with them of many things they will be interested to hear.'

'And the bomb?'

'We will dispose of it once I have disarmed. Now, please—' He jerked his head towards the rear of the lorry, and pointed towards Bates, still deep in conversation with Francisco. 'And her. Fast, please.'

Kyle nodded. He called over. 'Bates? Your carriage awaits.'

The harbour was almost deserted as the lorry lurched into gear. The same fisherman busy with his nets, an old lady walking a dog, but no one paid them much attention. Kyle wondered if the locals' indifference was deliberate, or merely the Spanish way; ask no questions.

The engine rumbled and the stink of diesel filled the air beneath the canvas canopy. Kyle grimaced as the lorry bumped along the uneven roads. Bates said, 'Do you think they're safe?'

'Francisco?'

'Yep.'

'Honestly?'

She gave him the look.

Kyle shifted his position on the hard bench and winced. 'I don't think anyone's safe.'

19

They passed through dusty villages, across a rickety iron bridge over a dry river bed and eventually turned off the main road onto a rutted track. After a short distance, Gordiovski coaxed the protesting engine up a steep incline into what looked like a deserted industrial yard. The vehicle came to a standstill beside a corrugated iron outbuilding. Kyle reckoned they were around thirty minutes from the coast. Another truck was parked alongside the outbuilding, a solid-framed lorry in much better shape than the one they'd just travelled in. A hired vehicle, perhaps – or maybe Yurichenko just wanted the best for his newly acquired explosive charge.

Beyond the yard lay the flat scrubland typical of the area, a rocky no man's land where only the hardiest plants and fauna could survive the blistering summer heat. Now, however, it was dusk and the heat of the day had receded to a more comfortable temperature. Despite this, Kyle was still perspiring when Gordiovski opened the tailgate and leaned into the truck's interior.

'Wait here.' The big man nodded. 'I will tell you when all is clear.'

Bates looked as though she wanted to say something,

perhaps object, but Kyle raised his hand to silence her. They watched Gordiovski and his tattooed crony walk towards the outbuilding.

When the shooting started Bates was first out. Kyle followed, rapidly discovering that adopting a limp favouring his left side was easier on his ribs. He was no match for Bates though; she covered the distance from their truck to the iron building in seconds.

The outbuilding's door was half off its hinges. Bates ducked through, ignoring Kyle's yell for caution. Swearing, he followed.

The interior was dark, the only illumination coming from the doorway through which they'd entered. Irregular shapes, the hulking outlines of abandoned machinery, were blacker silhouettes in the darkness. Kyle was happy to see them; they afforded cover.

More shots, a flare of brightness to his left, some distance away. It was a big warehouse. A voice called out, flat and harsh. 'Come out, comrade. There is no other exit.'

Gordiovski.

Crouching, Kyle moved along the warehouse's corrugated iron walls, warm to the touch after the day's heat. Where was Bates?

Another shot, this time from the opposite end of the building. Kyle hunkered down by one of the agricultural remnants, a tall rotivator-like structure with multiple spider-like legs.

Had Yurichenko brought the bomb into the warehouse? He would have needed help to do so; they'd been inside the interior of the Russian support ship at the time of Yurichenko's departure, so for all they knew he had a whole team with him? He would certainly have required assistance to transfer the bomb to the lorry at the harbour. And how had that been achieved without attracting attention? Kyle concluded that the harbour had been carefully chosen for that very reason. Sleepy, quiet, no one bothering too much about strangers.

Crack!

A bullet ricocheted off the rotivator a foot away from where he was crouched. He flinched. Without a weapon he was a sitting target, especially in the dark where he could be mistaken for anyone.

Keep moving...

He crept forward, something knocking against his foot. He bent and felt around, picked something up. A length of wood, an old broom handle maybe? He hefted it. It was better than nothing.

There was a faint shuffling noise somewhere ahead, a furtive movement. He turned. Then, from the other side of the warehouse, Gordiovski's voice. 'Show yourself, *Kapitan.*'

His command was followed by a frustrated crash of metal on metal; Gordiovski was getting impatient. A lighter shadow darted in front of him – he recognised the colour of Bates' shirt. A scuffle, he heard Bates cry out, and then nothing.

'No further, Mr Kyle.'

Yurichenko.

'My gun is against her head. Do not tempt me.'

Kyle whispered through dry lips. 'You can kill her, *Kapitan*, but it'll make no difference to the outcome. Gordiovski has no intention of arming the bomb.' He felt the wood in his hand, took a firmer grip. His night vision was improving; now he could see Yurichenko's outline squeezed into a corner, one hand over Bates' mouth, the other pressing a snub-nosed automatic against her skull.

'That's what he told you, eh?' Yurichenko's breath was rasping in his throat. The voice of a cornered man.

'You'll be treated fairly,' Kyle said. It was just talking. He moved a few inches closer.

'Not true,' Yurichenko said. 'No closer. Listen to me.'

'Been there, done that,' Kyle said. 'Still have the headache.'

'I am sorry for that.'

'No need for explanation. Your motives are clear.'

'No. You do not understand. I am not the threat here.'

Bates' muffled outrage was beginning to cause Yurichenko problems. He dug the automatic's barrel in harder. Kyle was close enough now to see her eyes, glittering pinpricks of repressed anger.

'It's not too late,' Yurichenko hissed. 'We can still stop him.'

Bates jerked her elbow into Yurichenko's stomach. She hadn't much leeway but she made the most of what she had. The Russian doubled over, relaxed his grip, and Kyle was straight in with the wood, swinging it at Yurichenko's head.

The Russian ducked but he wasn't quick enough. The broom handle caught him on the forehead and he fell against the corrugated wall. Kyle was watching the automatic, but he needn't have worried. Bates grabbed Yurichenko's wrist and twisted hard. The gun fell to the earthen floor and Kyle scooped it up. Yurichenko, clutching his head, sank to his haunches in defeat.

'My thanks, Mr Kyle.' He spun at the sound of Gordiovski's voice behind him. 'And Miss Bates, I thank you, also.'

Kyle ejected the automatic's magazine and dropped it on the floor, kicking it a few metres away from him. 'Enough shooting for one day. I think we're done here.'

'On the contrary, Mr Kyle.' Gordiovski adjusted the angle of his Kalashnikov until the nose was pointed directly at Kyle. 'We are just getting started.'

A cold thrill ran through Kyle's body from top to bottom, a physiological version of the nausea he had experienced at sea. 'Meaning?'

'Miss Bates, if you would, please?' Gordiovski pointed the

AK47 at Kyle's empty automatic. Bates took the gun from Kyle's nerveless fingers and retrieved the discarded magazine. She clipped it back into place and cradled the weapon in her palm. 'I'm sorry, Kyle, really I am.'

Kyle stared at Bates, and then back at Gordiovski, not understanding. Not wanting to understand.

'I warned you,' Yurichenko said quietly.

Gordiovski's tattooed tidier appeared like a ghost out of the gloom. 'All clear.'

'Good.' Gordiovski smiled, a wide, sardonic grin of satisfaction. 'Now we must get to work. Mr Kyle, my comrades will escort you to a place of safety until we are ready to depart.'

'Your comrades?' Kyle was still looking at Bates, hoping against hope.

She couldn't meet his gaze. 'Like I said, I'm sorry.'

'Spare me the apologies … *comrade*.'

Bates squared up to him. 'Did you really think I'd throw in my lot with the British Government after what they did to me? Kyle, you have *no* idea what I went through. And no one cared.'

'Until your lawyer buddy turned up? Is he a *comrade* too?'

'Does it matter?'

'It does to me.'

'He has … sympathies … with the Soviet cause, yes.'

Kyle nodded. 'And he got you thinking, what if?'

'Something like that.'

'So now you're going to drop a bioweapon on London? That's your response to being unfairly treated?'

She put her face close to his. Gordiovski and the tattooed guy were hovering, enjoying the exchange, the outpouring of Bates' fury and Kyle's bewilderment.

'Why the hell not?' Bates was in full flow. 'What do I owe my home country, where corrupt lawgivers locked me up for a crime I committed in self-defence? For the accidental killing of my attacker and would-be rapist – who, by the way, was one of Her Majesty's Government's most trusted employees, a senior police officer, for God's sake!'

There was nothing he could say. Nothing he could offer in return.

'I don't mean you any harm, Kyle. Fly the plane. That's it.'

'Sure, and you think Ygor here is going to let me walk off after the delivery? Take a bus home, go back to my normal life? Wake up, Bates.'

'He won't harm you.' Bates shot Gordiovski a hard look. 'He's given me his word.'

Kyle shook his head and Yurichenko let out a harsh guffaw.

'Enough,' Gordiovski stepped in, took Bates by the arm. 'Lock them up. I have work to do, and,' he pointed to his tattooed sidekick, 'so does Volchok.'

'You're taking orders from this clown?' The pounding in Kyle's head had redoubled, his eyes struggling to focus. A level nine was coming, and that meant trouble.

'Move, Kyle. And you.' Bates prodded Yurichenko with the automatic.

Kyle allowed himself to be led away. His nausea was back, and this time it wasn't seasickness.

20

The storeroom was just big enough for the two of them, or would have been, had it been empty. As it was, they shared the space with the detritus of the building's original function, possibly some kind of agricultural workshop. Which might have proved useful, had any of the objects in the cluttered space been heavy, sharp or dangerous. But they were rusted, old, broken, no use to either man nor beast.

Kyle wondered who had owned the place, what kind of labour might have been undertaken in the outbuilding's heyday. A repair facility for farming machinery, perhaps, or a maintenance workshop for agriculture, although what kind of agriculture might have been possible in the hills and extreme heat of southern Spain he wasn't entirely sure. It mattered little, however, given his present circumstances. What did matter was achieving some measure of physical recovery. He knew he was in a bad way. His ribs, his head and stomach were all competing for the top slot in Kyle's newly commissioned general-lack-of-wellbeing scale. His head was the clear front runner, hovering around an eight to nine. The only way to reduce this was by doing the one thing he couldn't afford to do right now: sleep.

'You look like shit,' Yurichenko offered from the other side of their small area of confinement.

Kyle looked up. There was a narrow tube light in the ceiling which illuminated the room in a dirty, fluorescent glow. From somewhere outside, in the main building, came the sound of clanking metal and the low murmur of male voices. He couldn't hear Bates, but that was just as well; he had nothing good to think about her. He took a slow, laborious breath.

'And that would be, let's see, whose fault exactly?'

Yurichenko sniffed. 'I apologise for the violence, but it was necessary to ensure that the bomb was salvaged according to plan. To have done otherwise would have raised Gordiovski's suspicions. And by the way—' He fingered his forehead, a dark bruise already visible and spreading fast. 'I think we're even.'

Kyle acknowledged this with a grunt. 'I reckon your pal had you figured out anyway.'

A pause. '*Da*. I underestimated him.' Another pause. 'And so, I think, did you, Mr Kyle.'

Kyle was more interested in Yurichenko's game plan than his own misplaced trust. 'What were you planning? After your team unloaded the bomb at the harbour? Was this the agreed location?'

'*Da*. I considered … making a run for it, is the phrase, yes? … when the sailors had returned to the support ship, once the bomb was on the truck, when I was alone. I would have had time; your interference created a delay for Gordiovski and an opportunity for myself. But—' He shrugged. 'I reasoned that it would be better to honour our existing arrangement, use the little time I had to disable the mechanism – not that I have a great deal of expertise in this, you understand, but I was willing to try.'

'How far did you get?'

'The mechanism is complex. With more time, maybe I

could have found a way, but this is not a task to be rushed, Mr Kyle.'

'Indeed not. But in any case Gordiovski suspected your intentions. He'd already sussed you out.'

Yurichenko looked puzzled.

'Trendy expression in the UK. Means he'd worked out what you were up to.'

'Ah. He was fast to arrive. He had, as you say, *sussed me out.*'

'If I'd known what you were planning... ' Kyle's frustration bubbled to the surface. 'If you had communicated your intentions, *Kapitan* ... I could have delayed him further, given you time. But I thought ... hell, I couldn't have predicted that Bates—'

'Ah, yes, Miss Bates. She has led you a ... what is the English expression? A merry jig?'

'Dance. Jig. Whatever.'

'You trusted her.'

'I had no reason not to. We've been through ... we've had some shared experiences. I thought...' He trailed off. 'It doesn't matter. Something happened to her, in prison. Something bad.' He rubbed his eyes with the heels of his hands, tried to refocus. 'Let's talk about you. What you told me, in the sub, it was true?'

'Da. All true.'

'And you wish to defect?'

Yurichenko thought for a moment. 'I have no choice. There is nothing left for me in Russia now.'

'If that lunatic drops his bomb on London there might not be much of anything left for anyone in Russia.'

'Russia will not be blamed. There is much ... ah, another English expression ... sleight of hand, that is correct?'

'Spot on. But blaming it on a minor terrorist group won't cover the truth forever. MI6 may have their failings, but they're methodical, and they're not entirely stupid.'

Yurichenko considered this for a few seconds. 'Yes,' he conceded. 'I think you may be right. Russian involvement will be exposed, maybe not immediately, but eventually.' He sighed. 'Gordiovski will do everything he can to complete his task. He is crazy enough, trust me. But he must not succeed.'

'Well, that'll be down to you and me, won't it?'

They lapsed into silence. After a while Yurichenko spoke again. 'It is almost nine. Gordiovski has much to do. I think you are safe to rest for at least a few hours.'

'I'm not arguing.' Kyle sighed resignedly, lay carefully back and closed his eyes. 'And if I were you, I'd follow your own advice.'

Exhausted as he was, however, Kyle found sleep elusive. The primary reason for this, of course, was Bates. A traitor? A double agent. It seemed preposterous to Kyle that the dutiful police detective he had met just a few years ago had not only thrown her hat in the ring with the Russians, but actually intended to drop a dirty bomb on England's capital city. It beggared belief. Was it really possible that she had become so angry, so disillusioned and hurt during her time in prison that her mindset had shifted gradually but inexorably from one ideology to another? Had she been so impressed by her smooth-talking, left-wing lawyer's expertise and his subtle indoctrination that she'd grabbed the opportunity to work for British Intelligence with both hands, a single, deadly purpose in mind? And – worse still – was that why she'd strung him along, dragged him into the whole sorry episode as an unwitting and unprepared understudy? Her voice echoed in his head, *You have reasons to be even madder this time around...*

Well, Miss Bates, I certainly have now. He clenched his jaw and regretted the action as a spasm of pain shot across his forehead. He peered at the dozing Russian, wondering what further internal damage the *Kapitan* might have inflicted. The bullet fragment, his own personal internal time bomb, could, even now, be just millimetres away from ending his life.

So what? No point worrying about it now…

He returned to the main issue; the bomb. Nothing else mattered. It had to be stopped. And it seemed they wanted him to fly the plane – which meant, logically, that they must be short of a pilot.

What could have upset their original plan? This, surely, would have included provision for someone to fly the transport plane. He recalled Bates speaking about a casualty, her erstwhile colleague. Had he also been working for the Russians? If so, why had he been killed? Was his demise the reason Bates had tasked Stanhope with finding an alternative?

He also wondered how she had known about his flying qualification? But then, he reasoned, Stanhope had seemed to know a great deal about him anyway. Why *wouldn't* they know?

Kyle shifted position until his ribs were as comfortable as they were ever going to be under the circumstances. Yurichenko was snoring softly. He should sleep too, but his mind had other ideas, innumerable thoughts tumbling over themselves, demanding his attention.

He had to break out, but what then? He had no idea how to defuse a bio-warhead. He could always drive off with it, as Yurichenko himself had considered, but he had no idea what his next move would be. Hole up somewhere and call the experts? What experts? Rural southern Spain was unlikely to be home to a random demographic of bioweapons experts.

Eventually, two words came into Kyle's bone-weary mind: safe disposal. The only alternative. But what was safe? Underwater had been a pretty good option, up to the point of salvage.

There was water between here and London.

It was a possibility. Of course, Gordiovski would be alert for any hint of sabotage, both before and after take-off. There was also Bates and the tattooed assistant to consider. Three against two – if they kept Yurichenko alive, which seemed to Kyle an unlikely prospect, although he hadn't voiced that opinion to the *Kapitan*.

Keep your eyes open, improvise, be alert.

He rested his head.

Kyle's eyes shot open. For a moment he was totally disoriented, but then another kick from Yurichenko brought him back.

'All right, cut it out. I'm awake.' He moved experimentally. His torso hurt, but the pain was manageable. His headache had reduced to somewhere around a three – also manageable. 'How long have I been out?'

'I cannot say. I, too, have slept.'

Kyle cast around the windowless room. There were no clues as to the time of day but, whereas before there had been industrious noises from outside their place of confinement, now there was deathly quiet. 'The wee small hours,' Kyle muttered.

'Three or four I think,' Yurichenko agreed. 'They also must sleep.'

'I wonder.' Kyle tried to imagine Gordiovski slumbering. It seemed unlikely. More likely the burly Russian would be watchful, waiting for first light and his big moment. 'They'll let us know when our presence is required,' he told Yurichenko. 'Rest while you can. It's going to be a long day.'

21

Bates raised her glass. *'Nostrovia!'* She downed the fiery liquid in one, wincing as the liquor stung her throat.

'Na, na.' Gordiovski shook his head. 'Not *nostrovia,* is *Na zdorovie!'* He drained his glass and shot her a leering grin. From the shadows, Volchok responded with a low chuckle. The tattooed man gave her the creeps. She could handle Gordiovski, but Volchok was a different species, the kind who would stab you in the back and not trouble himself to ask questions later. He was a fly in her ointment, but for now, all she could do was keep a wary eye on him.

'Another!' Gordiovski leaned over the packing case and waved the two-thirds empty bottle at her. Who knew what evil distillery had produced a spirit of such lethal strength. Her head was swimming after only three shots, but the potent concoction hardly appeared to be having any effect on Gordiovski. She was also keenly aware that Volchok was not partaking. He had explained his abstinence with three words, spoken with exaggerated clarity: 'An early job.' Bates interpreted this with a degree of disquiet. The 'job', she imagined, was likely to involve Francisco and his family. Loose ends.

'To our association, tomorrow and the future!' Gordiovski

sloshed more of the clear liquid into his own glass and also recharged hers. Pointless to refuse; it would only wind him up, make him argumentative. Bates preferred Gordiovski when he was drunk – as long as he was in a good mood. She raised her glass again. 'To Russia and all her people.'

'Rossija!' Gordiovski drank deeply.

Bates followed suit, but enough was enough. If she was to be of any use to anyone later in the night, she could not allow her blood-alcohol level to rise any further. Subterfuge would be necessary for the next and subsequent toasts which, she knew from experience, would inevitably follow.

The yard was still, the fire Volchok had built for them crackling softly in the brazier, sending sparks into the clear night sky. Her backside was numb from sitting on a hard packing case. She would make an excuse soon, take a few moments to relieve herself, and to think. She wondered how Kyle was. His injuries had looked painful, but he seemed to be mobile. He was still in the game. For now.

A game? She almost laughed aloud at her choice of word. What a game it had turned out to be. Lulled by the alcohol, her thoughts drifted back to the evening when everything had changed.

Up to that point, she had been a mere rookie, following Toby Pearce's every move, every instruction. She had been in awe of the senior agent she had been assigned to work with; his looks, his confidence, his experience. She had not thought to question either his motives or his decisions. In her mind's eye she could see him clearly, standing on the threshold of her hotel room, his deep set eyes twinkling with the prospect of action.

'Come on Bates. I know where our two friends are holed up. Time to give them a surprise, eh?'

She had followed without question, her heart beating fast as Pearce drove them along the coast towards Villaricos, pretty little Villaricos, with its harbour, modest scattering of lovingly-maintained fishing boats, expertly wound nets and other nautical paraphernalia lying unguarded on the quayside.

An unassuming house, a direct approach. Still, she did not question. The door was answered by a tall, handsome man in a white shirt and black trousers. He looked them up and down, smiled. 'Ah. The promised one.'

Even then she was unfazed; Toby knew what he was doing. She trusted him. They were led up a small staircase and into a bare room overlooking the harbour. A huge man in a vest was seated by the window, smoking and drinking some clear concoction from a cracked glass tumbler. He grunted as they came in. The handsome man pointed to a tatty settee. 'Sit.'

Toby Pearce looked at her and her stomach lurched as she spotted the momentary pang of regret that tightened his lips and creased his forehead.

'No choice, Bates. Sorry and all that.'

When she looked back at the man by the window, Gordiovski as she now knew him, he had an automatic cradled in his free hand. Bates sat down. The man by the window did not seem to be someone whose invitation you could decline, not safely.

Toby was still on his feet. He looked confident, pleased with himself. The big man spoke, almost casually.

'So, Mr Pearce – or Ajax, as we have come to know you. You are a man of your word, yes?'

Toby Pearce seemed irritated by the question. 'As you can see.' He waved a hand dismissively in Bates' direction and lit a cigarette.

Ajax. She'd heard that name, that codeword, used to refer to a double agent of British or maybe Dutch origin according to MI6 tracers, who was thought to be operating in Europe on behalf of the Russians. Toby Pearce was Ajax?

She moistened her lips, felt a rolling, sinking sensation in the pit of her stomach. Her fingernails dug into her palms. The handsome man sidled over, sat on the arm of the sofa. Although clearly in charge, he seemed tense, whereas the man by the window seemed relaxed, almost playful.

'I can see a little further than you imagine, Mr Pearce.'

Pearce dragged on his cigarette. 'Can you, Gordiovski? Can you really?'

'Or more accurately, our telephone tapping can.'

'Meaning?'

Bates summoned the courage to speak up. 'Toby, what in God's name have you done?'

Gordiovski turned to her, a gleam in his eye. 'Ah. She speaks. Come here, my little spy.'

'Be careful, Gordy.' The other man slipped from the arm of the sofa and stood between her and his subordinate.

'I am always careful, *Kapitan*,' Gordiovski replied. 'Which is why we know about Mr Pearce's calls home.'

'Calls home? What are you talking about?' Pearce was doing his best to affect nonchalance, but his sudden pallor told a different story.

Bates calculated how many steps she would require to get to the door. Too many. Way too many.

'Calls to your superiors in London, Mr Pearce.' Gordiovski drew a bead on Pearce, lined up the automatic's muzzle with the centre of his chest.

'Come on, you can't really believe that—'

'Evidence is evidence, Mr Pearce. You have played a dangerous game.'

'You promised me the money. On delivery. Well, here she is.' Pearce was babbling now, pointing frantically at Bates.

Gordiovski shook his head, smiling almost jovially. 'The *Kapitan* is not happy. He says you must be removed from the situation. For once, we are in agreement.'

'Quickly – and quietly, Gordy.' The other man, the *Kapitan*, nodded.

Somewhere outside a ship's klaxon broke the silence, its echo followed by the shrill, startled cries of circling gulls and the consumptive cough of a struggling nautical engine.

Gordiovski was screwing a silencer to the automatic's barrel with slow deliberation.

Toby Pearce's eyes were all movement. The window, the door, a weapon. Bates was paralysed, frozen in place on the battered sofa.

And then Gordiovski handed her the gun. 'If you please, Miss Bates.'

Her mouth fell open. 'What? No – I mean, I won't—'

Pearce was babbling. 'But I'm your only pilot, you can't do this without me. You can't. It's all planned, it's—'

Pearce wasn't begging, but it was a close call. His bluster, arrogance, patronising attitude were all gone, dissolving even further with every slow, desperate second.

The *Kapitan* had also conjured a weapon. He held it disdainfully, as though it were beneath him to contemplate its use. Nevertheless, the odds were now two armed against two not.

Gordiovski spun the automatic so that the butt was towards Bates. 'Take, please.'

'Bates, don't listen to him! He's bluffing—' Pearce's words stumbled perilously on, like a condemned man tiptoeing through a minefield.

Gordiovski prompted again with a grunt and a lift of his bushy eyebrows. Bates stood, found herself moving forward until the gun was pressed into her clammy hand.

'And now.' Gordiovski made an artificial gun with his fingers. 'Boom!'

Bates glanced at the *Kapitan*, but saw only cold, implacable assent.

'Either yourself, or him,' the *Kapitan* clarified. 'Please choose.'

Bates turned to face Toby Pearce. He backed away, both hands raised in front of him. 'Bates. Don't be so stupid. They'll kill you, too.'

'Maybe. Probably not,' Gordiovski said, swigging from his tumbler. 'We'll see.'

Bates raised the automatic, pointed it at Toby Pearce. Her mentor. Her colleague.

One more look at both Russians. No quarter given, no reprieve.

'Bates, please, you can't. I'm begging you—'

She closed her eyes.

Pulled the trigger.

22

Bates shuddered at the memory. Toby Pearce's stricken expression would haunt her to her last breath.

No choice. Him or me.

And then Gordiovski had thrown a cold glance to Yurichenko. She read it as though he had spoken aloud.

And now her?

And Yurichenko's thoughtful expression, the small shake of his head. 'We have lost our pilot, Gordy. Perhaps Miss Bates can assist us? Maybe even on a more permanent basis?'

There had followed a brief argument in Russian. It was obvious that Gordiovski wanted her dead. She shuddered again, reliving the paralysing helplessness of that moment.

But Yurichenko's logic had prevailed. Eventually he had turned to her with a smile: 'You will join us, Miss Bates?'

And her own voice, which she heard as though from the bottom of a deep well. 'Yes.'

Gordiovski at the window, drinking from the neck of a bottle, glaring.

'You are in another place, Miss Bates, I think.'

Bates started. Gordiovski was watching her, a sly smile playing about his lips. 'I wonder where you might be?'

'It's nothing,' she said. 'I'm tired, that's all.'

Gordiovski nodded. 'We leave at first light. Sleep until then.'

'What will you do with your *Kapitan*?'

'Not your business.' Gordiovski, drink in hand, cocked his head at something he'd heard in the distance – a motorbike, or scooter, zipping along the winding road below them. The sound grew louder until the machine roared into sight and skidded to a halt. A second, hard on the taillights of the first, also slewed to a standstill. The second rider dismounted, took his place behind the first rider and the bike accelerated away again. Volchok and Gordiovski exchanged a look.

Bates coughed as dust and exhaust fumes caught in her throat. The deposited motorcycle could have only one purpose: Volchok's transport for his 'cleaning' operation. She summoned her courage, glared at Gordiovski. 'I'd appreciate an answer.'

'Like I say,' the Russian growled. 'Not your business.'

'I'm working with you, so I'd challenge that,' Bates said.

'You hear that, Nikolai?' Gordiovski grinned at Volchok. 'She would challenge me.' He wagged his finger, slowly, deliberately. 'Miss Bates, you work *for* me, not *with* me, understand? For now, your job is to make sure that Mr Kyle is compliant.'

The two men switched to Russian, their voices low. Volchok laughed at some quip Gordiovski had made.

She needed to understand their intentions. Kyle would fly, but what then? The *Kapitan* ... well, anything was possible, but she didn't reckon Gordiovski would allow a potential defector to walk away. She watched Gordiovski pour yet another large measure into his glass. His capacity was staggering. Surely he must sleep eventually?

She pursed her lips. Best bide her time, wait for Volchok to leave.

But Francisco, Camila…

She had a responsibility to the family. Surely she should at least try to warn them?

Too dangerous …

Her eyelids were growing heavy. If they closed, she knew she would return to the night of Pearce's death.

Murder, Jude. Pearce's murder…

Surely not murder? She'd had no choice; it was practically self-defence. Manslaughter at best.

Ah, manslaughter again. Getting to be a habit, Jude…

She bit down hard on her lip.

Think! DI Patterson deserved what he got. That really was self-defence…

And a small voice whispered, *You paid the penalty, though, Jude. Three years inside, remember?*

No need for reminders.

But you got through it, right? Just like you'll get through this.

The combination of heat from the brazier's embers, and the effects of the alcohol were hypnotising her so that the two Russians seemed ephemeral, insubstantial shapes in the shadows.

Her eyes closed.

Pearce's body, lying at full stretch. The blood. Her hands, shaking as the *Kapitan* took the automatic from her. And her words, shaky, whispered.

'Yes. I can find you a replacement pilot.'

An imperceptible nod from the *Kapitan*. 'We have a new Ajax, Gordy.' A gesture to Pearce's body. 'Dispose, please.' And to her, a penetrating look. 'You stay here. We make plans.'

Bates jerked awake. She was alone.

Idiot, Bates, idiot…

Where was Gordiovski? Volchok? She scanned the empty

yard but there was no sign of them.

Rubbing her stiff limbs she crept to the warehouse, inched along its length, stuck her head round the corner. Still nothing.

Strong hands grabbed her from behind, held her arms. Kyle's voice spoke in her ear, low and angry.

'Follow the leader, Bates. And—' he hissed in her ear, 'just for the record, yep, I am *really* mad now.' She felt cold metal press into the thin skin above her ear.

'Giza mode?' She allowed herself to be shoved ahead, along the length of the warehouse frontage.

'And then some.'

23

'An hour till first light,' Kyle said.

'You feel better, no?'

Kyle considered the *Kapitan's* question. The headache was still at three. He probed his ribs and winced. He rolled slowly onto his good side and carefully found his feet. Not bad. Not ideal, but he could move, at least. 'Could be worse.'

'Good. Then we turn our attention to escape. I suggest you deal with Gordiovski. I will attend to the vehicle.'

'Thanks. Short straw accepted.' Kyle was examining their prison. There was one door, and a window space that had been sealed with some kind of cement or filler. He grabbed a length of discarded piping and made a few exploratory scrapes, but it was solid.

Beneath it, however, the corrugated iron had rusted in places along the iron frame. He probed further, searching for signs of weakness, but the rusted areas were too small to be of any use. 'Take more time than we've got,' he muttered and gave one final shove on the pipe. It slipped through a hole in the rusted metal and something on the other side caught hold of it, moved it back towards him. Kyle let go.

What?

Another tool, some kind of improvised jemmy, appeared in

its place, began to work up and down the crack. The rust crackled and popped as it was displaced, and a widening slit began to open up beneath the frame. The tool disappeared and Kyle put his eye gingerly to the hole. A voice in heavily accented Spanish hissed through the gap. 'Wait. I get something else.'

Francisco.

By now, Yurichenko was also taking an interest in proceedings. Kyle raised his hand for silence. Too much noise already and he didn't want to add to it, far less draw Gordiovski's or Bates' attention.

More scrabbling outside. Something was clamped to the corrugations beneath the frame, and they watched as the metalwork was gradually peeled back, like a tin-opener circumnavigating a tin of tomatoes.

An engine roared in the darkness. A motorbike, close by. The implement froze, and then recommenced with greater urgency as the sound of the engine swelled then faded into the distance. Francisco's face appeared, dark, sweat-grimed, urgent.

'*Rápidamente!*'

Kyle squeezed out first, followed by Yurichenko. They followed Francisco at a crouch to the far end of the warehouse. There was a brazier burning low in the yard, someone sitting just within the warm radius of its light. Bates. She looked to be alone. Where was Gordiovski? Better to have the giant in view than have to speculate on his whereabouts. Yurichenko was headed around the corner, looking for a way in. Francisco grabbed his arm. '*Una puerta – una oficina.*'

'A door – I think,' Kyle said.

'*A la izquierda.*' Francisco nodded, gestured with his left hand.

'On the left?' Kyle interpreted. 'Francisco – the motorbike. *Moto...*' He mimicked an accelerator wrist movement. 'I think the Russian goes to your family. You must be there.'

Apprehension clouded the Spaniard's face. '*¿Si? ¿Mi familia? ¿Los Rojos?*' He spat. '*Luché en la guerra civil. Los mataré a todos.*'

Yurichenko grinned. 'He says he fought in the civil war. He will kill them all.'

'Thank you, Francisco,' Kyle shook his hand. 'Go, now.' He frowned. 'You have transport? *¿Transporte?*'

'*Si, si. Dos en una moto. Maté a los dos.*'

Kyle was taken aback. 'Did I hear that right? You killed them? *¿Dos hombres?*'

'*Si. Dos. Tengo la moto.*'

'Yes. And now he has transport,' Yurichenko translated. 'I must go to the lorry, the bomb.'

Kyle was wondering who Francisco had killed. Not Gordiovski, surely?

But before he could voice the question, Francisco had gripped his shoulder briefly in farewell and disappeared into the darkness. Yurichenko, too, had crept forward towards the door Francisco had indicated. Kyle hesitated. Could he trust the *Kapitan*?

More importantly, where *was* Gordiovski? Either the big man or Volchok had just ridden away. Kyle's money was on Volchok. The tidier.

Either way, he was on his own now. He crept on, past the doorway through which Yurichenko had just disappeared. An office, maybe? Which would lead into the interior. Kyle left him to it and kept moving. He wanted a chat with Bates.

On his own terms.

24

'It's not what you think, Kyle.'

'Now, where have I heard that before?' He maintained his half nelson grip on her arm, prodded her slim neck with the length of piping.

'Where are we going? There's nothing out there except scrub and a few wildcats.'

'Just keep walking.'

'Look, I was in an impossible position.'

'Oh, really?' She stumbled and Kyle tightened his grip. He spoke in her ear. 'So you created one for me as well, just to make us even?'

'Toby sold me out.'

'Who the hell is Toby?'

She dug her heels into the hard ground, leaned into him. 'Your predecessor, that's who.'

Kyle shoved her. 'Walk.'

They were at the edge of the quadrangle. Ahead lay an indistinct slope of, as Bates had predicted, hard, scrubby earth, dotted here and there with the squat shapes of hardy plants and stunted bushes. He could see why Gordiovski and his compatriots had chosen the location. It was the archetypal middle of nowhere.

From the direction of the road the staccato of a revving bike engine broke the silence. Bates turned to look, but Kyle prodded her forward. 'Not your concern, Bates. Keep going.'

He silently wished Francisco well; Volchok had a head start.

A split second later, from inside the warehouse, an echoed response, a blast of diesel-fuelled anger; Yurichenko.

And hard on its heels, a fusillade of small arms fire; Gordiovski.

Kyle grabbed Bates, pushed her to the ground, covered her body. At any moment the lorry would burst out of the warehouse and more bullets would follow.

They lay together, breathing hard.

Nothing.

Silence, apart from the lorry's engine, idling now, turning over in its designed sequence of ordered explosions, still in neutral, still apparently stationary.

'This is more complicated than you think, Kyle.' Bates' voice was muffled, but as usual she was determined to make her point.

'Quiet. I don't fancy collecting another bullet – that's as complicated as this gets. Get up.' He grabbed her collar.

From the far side of the warehouse, more shots rang out.

'Lorry. Go.' Kyle reestablished the half-nelson and moved forward, keeping them fast and low.

'Listen, you don't know the half of this,' Bates gasped as he shoved her towards the warehouse door.

'I know enough.' He could hear the lorry's engine still ticking over. With any luck he could finish what Yurichenko had started while Gordiovski was busy.

They reached the entrance, and holding Bates firmly by the arm, Kyle stuck his head into the gap.

The blow caught him on his left bicep, a paralysing, numbing shock. He dropped the piping. Bates spun around, dipped and scooped it up. Gordiovski stepped into the oblong of light cast into the warehouse interior by the pre-dawn light. Kyle didn't even check for the Kalashnikov; he knew it was there. He leaned against the warehouse wall and massaged his arm. Bates hefted the piping, nodded to Gordiovski who gave a satisfied grunt.

'Good. If he moves, hurt him.' The Russian handed Bates a pistol that Kyle recognised as a Makarov 9mm.

Would she use it? Not to incapacitate him – he was their pilot, after all, and surely their past connection, however compromised, would cause her to hesitate? Kyle let his shoulders drop. Better they thought him beaten.

But where was Yurichenko? Looked like he'd got clean away.

And it looked like flying was still on the agenda.

Francisco willed the machine to go faster. He would not allow anything to happen to his *familia*. It was unthinkable. *Los Rojos, los bastardos…*

He took a corner too fast and the machine skidded, almost slipped away from him. He glanced left. The sea, far below, the rocks.

Ten cuidado, Francisco…

The sun was a red disc, rising slowly like a creature of light from the ocean depths. This was his country, his land, his water. *Los Rojos* … they had no business here. What he had done he had done to protect Camila, Arianna. He glanced at his wristwatch as he sped past the familiar landmarks.

Dies minutos…

Tiny flutters of panic clutched at his heart like the over friendly shoals of *sardinas* who liked to brush against his skin as he swam beside his boat. Camila had laughed with delight when they had done the same to her.

Papi, mi están haciendo cosquillas!

He bent over the handlebars, opened the throttle.

25

Camila was half-awake. She had slept fitfully, knowing that Papa had gone out. He was not fishing. He was doing something dangerous. That much she knew.

She swung her legs out of bed and went to her bedroom window, where thin sunlight was filtering through the vertical gap between her curtains. A new day was beginning, but her heart was full of foreboding. *Los Rojos* had let her and her Papa go, but, as well as Papa, she also feared for the lady and the man who had helped her. The woman, Bates, was nice. She had wanted to help Papa and Mama – that much was clear. And the man, too, her friend, the tall one with the kind eyes; he had gone with the Russian, Gordy. That wasn't good.

Camila went through to the kitchen and drew herself a glass of water. Perhaps Mama would let her go for a swim with Maria today. But Mama was worried and sad; she would probably want Camila to stay home again. That was OK, though. Mama shouldn't be sad; Camila resolved that she would make her happier, somehow.

She finished her water, rinsed the glass. She stood at the kitchen window, looking out on the tiny square of garden where Mama worked with her pots and seeds. Mama loved her garden, and Camila enjoyed helping whenever she could. She loved the tiny cactii with their needled-sharp spines and green, waxy stems, the vibrant pinks and reds of hibiscus and oleander. Best of all, though, was when Papa was home and they would sit outside on the bench in the cool of the evening, Papa with his *cerveza*, Mama with her *naranja* and Camila with a cold glass of *limonada*.

Thinking about Mama's orange juice made her think about breakfast. Mama deserved a treat. Camila set to work. She found olive oil and tomatoes to make Mama's favourite *tostado*, poured ice-cold *naranja* into a clean glass. When Papa came back she would make him something special, too.

After a few minutes of preparation Camila went to see if her mother was awake but she found Arianna still fast asleep, her dark hair spread across the pillow, one arm thrown carelessly over the top sheet. Camila smiled. Mama should rest. She was tired and worried. She would bring her breakfast soon.

Camila returned to the kitchen, but then her ears pricked up as a sound reached her from outside, soft at first but growing louder. *La moto…*

Papá!

She went to the front door and unfastened the chain, her heart beating with excitement. The morning sun shone into the living room and onto her expectant face. There was a small gap in the wall of their front yard through which anyone walking by could be momentarily glimpsed before they came into full view. Camila glued her eyes to the spot.

And froze.

It was not Papa.

It was the man with the painted arms from the boat.

Camila softly closed the door and backed into the house.

¿Que hacer?

She heard the surreptitious footsteps moving around the

perimeter of the house. Like the big man before, he would try to come in through an open window.

Pero estoy despierta…

Camila padded into the back bedroom, the spare room, where Papa kept his special things. She wasn't really allowed in here, but Papa wouldn't be angry with her, surely, not now? Not when she was trying to protect Mama.

She began searching for something she knew Papa kept in this room. Mama did not like it, but Papa always said he would never throw it away. He said he kept it *por respeto* for his friends who had died in the war. Mama sometimes said it was dangerous, a bad thing to have in the house. Papa frowned when she said this, looking angry and hurt, and Mama always backed down. They all knew it was special for Papa.

She opened a cupboard door, revealing only stacks of old books and papers, and then she tried the wardrobe where Papa's old clothes hung in rows, like bats in a cave. She rummaged in the depths, her hands looking for cold metal.

Nothing.

Somewhere in the house she heard a *click*.

Her heart began to beat faster. She went to the single bed, pulled up the coverlet, looked underneath.

There.

She carefully pulled the rifle from its hiding place. Papa had shown it to her once before, to satisfy her *curiosidad.*

It was heavy.

Camila hefted the rifle, her small hands feeling for the trigger. Something was wrong, she knew. She peered at the gap at the bottom of the rifle.

This is where the bullets go, see? In here, Papa had shown her. *You must never touch this, mi chica inteligente. You must promise, eh?*

But there were no bullets, she could see. There was a

special box you pressed them inside, but where was it?

She set the rifle down carefully, taking care to point the end away from her, just in case, and searched under the bed. Her fingers scrabbled on the dusty floor, this way and that.

Just outside the bedroom something moved, a near-silent shuffle of feet. Camila stifled a sob, redoubled her efforts. Her hand closed around a small rectangular object; Papa had called it a *cargador*. She knew just where it went – into that gap underneath the gun.

But when she tried to push it in it wouldn't fit. With shaking hands she tried again. It wouldn't go.

The door knob moved, turning slowly with a small squeak. *Like a mouse...*

Don't think crazy thoughts. Think clever thoughts, clever thoughts, clever thoughts ...

Then she remembered. You had to pull the thing at the end. It would stay out, then you could put the bullets in.

She heaved at the bolt. It came back easily, clicked, and Camila clipped the magazine into place.

Now push it, see, like this... She could hear Papa's voice so clearly, as though he was here with her.

The bolt slid back. She followed its movements with her hand as it locked into place.

Now it is very dangerous...

Yes, Papa...

The door opened. The man with the bald head and arm pictures was standing in the hall. He was holding a small, black pistol. It looked like a toy, with its fat cigar-shaped barrel. Camila registered the surprised look on the bald man's face as she pointed Papa's gun at him and pulled the trigger

The rifle went off with a crack like the fireworks at the festival *di fuegos* and the wooden stock banged into her shoulder, throwing her against the bed. The room filled with a horrible smell of smoke that stung her eyes and made her cough. Her shoulder hurt; it felt like it was broken. Now she would be in trouble. She lay still and wondered what the man would do next.

But the man was also lying still, and a red river was spreading towards her across the tiled floor. Mama was standing over him, her hand covering her mouth. She kept looking at the man, then at Camila, then at the man again.

Camila did not move; her shoulder hurt too much to move. And then, somehow, Papa was there, gathering her into his arms. He was crying.

Mi chica inteligente, oh dios, dios! Mi chica inteligente...

26

Kyle grimaced as the lorry bounced over a pothole. He was tired, hungry, in pain and deeply pissed off. Nothing made sense. Or maybe he was just stupid, and everything was obvious. Maybe his brain had simply ceased to function since Yurichenko's elbow to the temple.

Think, Kyle, think...

What *did* he know? He was expected to fly an aircraft to England, to London, for the purposes of releasing a biological weapon over the city. Two adversaries, Gordiovski and ... and –this was still hard to say – and Bates. Two to one. Not bad odds. Maybe Gordiovski counted as two. Three to one, then. Still not so bad. But he himself was hardly a one. More like a half.

The temperature was slowly rising in his airless prison, and the recovered bomb, cradled in its iron dolly, was a constant reminder of the severity of his situation. He was tied securely to one of the internal struts, but even unrestrained he wouldn't have had a clue how to render the warhead unusable, or even if such a thing were possible.

The lorry continued to rumble onwards, lurching from time to time as the wheels encountered ruts and pot holes. By the time they finally came to a halt, Kyle's tongue was stuck to the roof of his mouth and his head was pounding its way to a six.

He heard the tailgate being unlocked, and then light flooded in.

'Water. I swung it in your favour.' Bates clambered up and handed him a plastic bottle of lukewarm water.

He downed it in one. 'You're all heart.'

'He wants to keep you compliant.' Bates nodded towards the driver's cab.

'I'll bet he does.'

Bates leaned in close. 'Just trust me, Kyle.' Her voice was a whisper as she untied his wrists.

'Been there, done that.'

She shot him a warning look as Gordiovski shambled to the rear of the lorry and peered in, his small, pig-like eyes suspiciously scanning the interior before settling on Kyle.

'You come.'

Kyle climbed out and made a show of stretching his legs, rubbing his wrists where the steel cord had bitten into his flesh. The sun was beating down on what appeared to be a barren landscape. He saw nothing but untilled soil, weeds and scrub – and a twin-engined aeroplane parked conveniently a few metres away. Beyond this, a tall perimeter fence stretched from east to west. It was too far away for him to read the signs, but it was pretty obvious what they were for.

'This is the zone, right? Where the first bomb fell?'

Gordiovski didn't answer – he was too busy unfastening the metal clamps holding the dolly securely in position – but Bates nodded. 'Yep.'

'So it's radioactive?'

'Not so much that it'll harm you. It's fenced off as a precaution. The Yanks already had one pass at cleaning it up.'

'You – Bates, come.' Gordiovski beckoned with his

customary growl.

She bent to help him.

Kyle was thinking. The forbidden zone. Made sense. No one would disturb them here. 'And the plane?'

'A CASA C-212. An STOL,' Bates called over her shoulder as she worked to help Gordiovski with the dolly.

'Short take off and landing? Never flown one.'

Bates paused, hands on hips. 'How hard can it be? It has wings, two propellers.'

'I admire your faith in my abilities.'

'Just come over here and give us a hand, would you?'

Easing the dolly from the truck and rolling it over the uneven ground did indeed prove to be a three-person job, although loading it into the interior of the C-212 via the transport plane's rear ramp and pulley proved considerably easier. As he worked, he contemplated making a run for it but, as before, there was nowhere to go. In his weakened state he might not even make it as far as the fence, let alone to any place of refuge. And even if he did manage to escape Gordiovski's clutches, what then? The Russian would simply find an alternative pilot to carry out the mission. It might take time, but that's what would happen.

And Kyle couldn't allow that.

When the dolly was finally aboard, Gordiovski busied himself fastening it securely in place, while Kyle sat on the ramp, mopped his brow and thought about Bates. Her whispered confidence in the truck had been as unexpected as it had been discombobulating.

Trust me.

What on earth was she up to?

'Kyle – food.' She appeared at his side as though conjured by his thoughts, handed him a packet of sandwiches and another bottle of water.

'You've thought of everything.'

She gave him a withering look. 'Just eat. Airborne by noon. That's the plan. When you're finished, I suggest you go up front and familiarise yourself with the controls.'

'Sure. My pleasure.'

She held his gaze for a fraction too long, and then spoke two words which changed everything.

'Be ready.'

She walked away. Kyle watched her open-mouthed, the food and drink forgotten.

Familiarise yourself with the controls…

Probably good advice.

27

Kyle examined the flight manual. Max speed 230 mph. Max ceiling 10,000 feet.

'That's OK.' Bates' voice came from behind the pilot's seat. 'You'll be flying well below 10,000.'

'She's bigger than I've ever flown before.'

'Same principles apply, I assume.'

Kyle moistened his lips. It had been months since he'd flown, and then only in a borrowed Cessna 150.

'How long?' Gordiovski, sweaty, impatient, crammed into the cockpit behind them.

'Thirty minutes,' Kyle said. 'You'd prefer me to be confident that I can fly this thing, right?'

'Have you eaten?' Bates addressed the Russian before he could find a sarcastic rejoinder. 'Thought not. Sandwiches and water only, I'm afraid.' She handed him a package like the one Kyle had received.

Gordiovski took the food without a word and settled into the bucket seat, tore open the wrapping and began to eat.

'I'll leave you to it, Kyle,' Bates said. 'Last minute checks to attend to.'

'I'll bet.' Kyle didn't look up, turned another page of the manual. The words danced in front of his exhausted eyes.

It was doable; as Bates said, same principles. A shorter take off than he was used to, a heavier aircraft, but he was reasonably confident he could handle it. The instruments were self-explanatory, as were the controls.

The real question was whether to wait on Bates and her instruction to be ready, or to take matters into his own hands. Whatever happened, he had no intention of flying anywhere near London, and preferably nowhere near land. His primary focus was how to manage this without arousing Gordiovski's suspicions.

'I'm starting her up,' he said to no one in particular.

The engines roared obediently into life. 'So far, so good.' He turned to solicit Gordiovski's approval.

The big Russian was sprawled in the bucket seat, head thrown back, his chest rising and falling in the regular rhythm of deep sleep.

Bates appeared at his side. She lifted the Russian's wrist, checked his pulse, allowed herself a brief smile of satisfaction.

Kyle removed his headset. 'This is the part where I trust you?'

'Yes.'

Bates lifted each of Gordiovski's eyelids, muttered approvingly to herself. 'He's out.'

Kyle watched her as she pinched the Russian's hands. Gordiovski made no response.

'What did you give him?

'It doesn't matter. What does matter, though, is that we get going before he comes to. We just have to wait for Yurichenko.' She consulted her watch. 'He should be here anytime.'

Kyle shook his head. 'I give up.' He replaced the headset, made a small adjustment. 'You'll brief me in your own good time?'

'It's complicated, Kyle.'

'I wish people would stop telling me that.'

'We have to get him to London in one piece.'

Kyle swivelled to face her. 'And what about that?' He made an open-handed gesture towards the bomb, nestled in its securing brackets, nose pointing at the rear cargo ramp.

'It doesn't matter,' she said. 'It's not a problem.'

He struggled to make sense of what, on the face of it, seemed a ludicrously dismissive statement. 'It's not a pro—?'

They were interrupted by a screech of brakes. Bates dropped Gordiovski's hand. 'Here he is. Take off asap, please.'

Kyle peered from the cockpit window in time to see Yurichenko slamming the door of a dusty and battered-looking SEAT 600. He raised his hand in greeting. Kyle waved back.

Yurichenko climbed on board via the rear ramp and Kyle found the switch to close it. The Russian *Kapitan* came forward immediately to check on Gordiovski. 'Out cold.' He nodded approvingly. 'Good job.'

'Sit down and and buckle up,' Kyle said. 'And then maybe someone would be kind enough to fill me in once we get underway.'

'Of course.' For once, Bates looked penitent. 'Sorry for the subterfuge. How're you feeling, by the way?'

'I'll live. Just let me get this thing in the air.'

He ran through the standard checks: flight controls, altimeter, directional giro, fuel gauges, trim, flaps. He worked through the recommended list, remembering most from his training and learning a few more specific to the C-212. All seemed fine. The landing area ahead was flat and clear.

Parking brake off. Check.

Kyle took a deep breath and opened the throttle.

28

'Put this on.' Kyle handed Bates a headset. 'Hear me OK?'

'Yep.' Bates made a small adjustment, repositioned her microphone.

'Start talking.' Kyle's eyes were all over the instruments. All good so far. Height 8,000 feet. The plane handled well for her bulk; he'd expected to have to drag her across the sky, but she only required the lightest of touches. 'And keep an eye out for the Spanish air force. We won't be on their radar as a scheduled flight.'

'That's taken care of.' Her voice crackled in his headset.

'Of course it is.' Kyle nodded. 'Silly of me.'

'Cleared from London. The Spanish know all about it.'

'Good to hear. Being shot down would make my day a whole lot worse.'

'This is a joint op, Kyle, London and Moscow. Our job is to get the asset back to the UK in one piece. After that, it's out of our hands. Job done.'

'Gordiovski.'

'Yes.'

'Why?'

Bates glanced behind her. Gordiovski's state was unchanged. Yurichenko sat behind the big Russian, eyes closed, recharging.

'We did a deal. Gordiovski was getting too powerful for the Kremlin's comfort. He's assembled what amounts to a private army on the outskirts of Moscow, and he has senior KGB contacts in his pocket too scared to challenge him. Sakharovsky went into panic mode. They had to find a way to get to Gordiovski but couldn't get close to him in Moscow. Gordiovski's too clever – his security is watertight.'

'Sakharovsky?'

'Ex-head of KGB. He came up with a solution; find a carrot that would appeal to Gordiovski's ambitions, intercept him, get him to London where he'll be debriefed and his teeth drawn.'

'The bomb.'

'Yes. Sakharovsky reasoned that the idea of a dirty bomb would appeal to Gordiovski's baser instincts, and he was right. He also calculated that he might be open to the suggestion of an escalation of the threat.'

'From Spain to London.' Kyle nodded again. 'Smart guy.' He glanced at the altimeter; just under 10,000 feet. They'd reached their ceiling. Any higher and they'd need oxygen. Apart from a wide cumulus forming to the north-west the sky was clear, which was still more than could be said for Kyle's understanding. 'What do we get in return for delivering Gordiovski?'

'Good question.' Bates looked pleased. 'Sakharovsky agreed to release one of ours. I can't say much more.'

Kyle was thinking. 'Where does Yurichenko fit into this?'

'He wants to defect, pure and simple. But he's here in an official capacity, as far as the Kremlin is concerned – to facilitate our delivery.'

'So the bomb is a dud?

'Not entirely. It's similar to the ones the US has already recovered, so in its present state it's only a potential radioactive threat. On the other hand, if it's armed...'

Kyle winced. 'I get it. And Gordiovski is unaware of this?' Kyle frowned. It seemed careless on Gordiovski's part.

'He was fed misinformation which he had no reason to disbelieve, and the arming mechanism is identical. But he did eventually figure out that Yurichenko's agenda didn't exactly align with his.'

'Hence his apparent loyalty switch on the ship? That was for my benefit, correct? He wanted me onside to help him apprehend Yurichenko.'

'You're getting there, Kyle.'

'Good to know.' Kyle checked airspeed and fuel levels for the umpteenth time. 'And you?'

'I knew it wasn't a bioweapon.'

'I don't mean that. I mean you. Your allegiances.'

'Toby Pearce was playing a double game. Stanhope guessed. Pearce tried to make amends but it was too late. Gordiovski became suspicious that he'd turned back to London – which, of course, he had. They tapped his phone.'

'What happened to him?'

Bates looked at the floor.

'I'll ask another time.' He changed tack. 'And the reason you didn't tell me all this to begin with?'

She looked up. 'Would you have agreed to come, to help – without the bioweapon threat?'

He thought for a moment. 'Yes, because it was strongly hinted that you might be in trouble.'

She was quiet for a few seconds, then a brief smile. 'I'm flattered.'

They flew on in silence. Kyle's headache had reduced to a two, pretty much as good as it ever got. His ribs still ached, but provided he didn't make any sudden moves he could cope. He was thinking hard, reviewing the events of the past twelve hours methodically, thoughtfully.

The revelation that Bates was on the level was a huge relief, but something had shaken her. Something had happened between her and the treacherous Toby Pearce, and he was pretty sure he knew what that something was. A test of allegiance, Gordiovski's stark solution...

I was in an impossible position...

And then there was Yurichenko. He talked a good story; he'd certainly pulled the wool over Kyle's eyes, and that still rankled. The *Kapitan* had made sure the bomb had been successfully recovered – and then he'd taken the device to the warehouse, with assistance, but without Gordiovski.

Kyle glanced at Bates, but she was dozing, her chest rising and falling. Best let her sleep.

Kyle assumed the *Kapitan* had been caught tinkering with the mechanism. Whatever he'd been doing, his actions had been suspicious enough for Gordiovski and his pal Volchok to start firing, no questions asked. Gordiovski had assumed attempted sabotage – but if Yurichenko had known the bomb was harmless – radiation leaks aside – until armed, and not a dangerous bioweapon, what would explain his actions? Why would he even concern himself with the bomb's internal mechanism?

Unless he intended to arm it, of course. But that made no sense, either, given what Bates had told him.

Kyle glanced at the altimeter, ran through a series of in-flight checks. The Atlantic and the Spanish coastline to his left; to his right, the snow-capped Pyrenees. He made an effort to relax his shoulders, allow the tension to dissipate. This was just a short flight, followed by a welcome committee of some sort, a handover, a return to normality – or so he assumed. What would they do with the bomb? Would they ship it to the US? Stanhope would no doubt have plans in place to lever every possible political advantage from the operation.

Kyle took a deep breath. Not his problem. He adjusted the radio volume and began to pay closer attention to air traffic. He would need to identify their intended flight path soon. Bates hadn't divulged their final destination, but he imagined they'd be heading to a small airfield, as far away as practicable from prying eyes.

He sensed a movement behind, half-turned to check all was well, expecting to see two slumbering Russians.

What he actually saw was Gordiovski, disoriented, bleary-eyed, but halfway out of his seat. Before Kyle could react, Gordiovski was on his feet and spoiling for a fight.

29

Kyle unclipped his belt and headset, alerting Bates as he did so. 'Take the controls.'

Bates' mouth widened into an alarmed O. '*What*? I don't know how t—'

'Just hold her steady.' With that, Kyle flung himself at Gordiovski.

Gordiovski let out his breath in a roar, parried Kyle's attempted punch. The aeroplane yawed to port, tipping Kyle against the fuselage.

'Kyle! I can't do this!' There was panic in Bates' voice as she yelled above the noise in the cockpit.

Yurichenko had ducked out of harm's way and was sprawled on the floor. He made it to all fours before the plane dipped and rolled him forward.

Kyle was trying to stay out of range of Gordiovski's hammer-blow fists. Even half-doped, the strength of the man was extraordinary.

An automatic had magically appeared in Yurichenko's hand. 'Enough!'

Gordiovski registered the loss of his advantage, let his arms drop to his sides. His moth twisted into a frustrated snarl.

'I will kill you if I have to, Gordy.'

Kyle believed him.

'This man has done me great harm.' Yurichenko was breathing heavily and leaning on the seat backrest, but he kept Gordiovski in his sights. 'He and his associates are the architects of my humiliation. They covered their tracks well, as they always do, but I spared no expense, financial or personal, to get to the truth.'

The plane banked sharply to the left, dipped her nose. Kyle steadied himself against the back of the co-pilot's seat.

'Kyle!'

'Keep your airspeed up, gently ease back on the controls.' Kyle spoke calmly but kept his eyes all the while on Gordiovski. 'You're doing great, Bates.'

Yurichenko made a gesture with the nose of the automatic. 'Please, take the controls, Mr Kyle. Miss Bates? The drugs. Do *not* move.' This to Gordiovski, who had taken a step towards his ex-partner. 'I will shoot you, Gordy, make no mistake.'

'In my bag. Below my seat.' Bates' reply was through gritted teeth. 'Fast would be good.'

'I'll look.' Kyle bent and rummaged on the floor for Bates' bag.

'Hurry, Kyle, for God's sake…'

'What's our height?'

'3,000 feet. Just under.'

'That's OK.' His scrabbling hands closed around a syringe. He took it out, examined it. It was loaded.

Bates glanced sideways. 'Give it all to him. He's had half already. Not enough, obviously.'

Kyle squeezed between the seats into the hold, held the syringe up for Gordiovski's inspection. 'Better than a bullet, Gordiovski.'

Gordiovski's eyes were pinpoints of murder. He looked at Kyle, then at the unwavering gun held in Yurichenko's steady hand. He held out his arm.

'Good.' Kyle jabbed the needle into Gordiovski's muscular bicep. 'I'd sit, if I were you.'

Gordiovski dropped heavily into his seat, his eyes already closing.

Kyle held onto the rail as the plane yawed again. 'You can put the gun away.'

Yurichenko gave a terse shake of his head. 'I do not think so. A change of plan. You will fly to new co-ordinates.'

'Excuse me?'

'*Kyle*! I'm losing this...'

'Just do what I tell you, and all will be well.' Yurichenko managed to get to his feet as the aircraft swayed from side to side as though in a heavy crosswind.

'I'll fly where we're intended to fly,' Kyle said. 'As scheduled. You'll be treated fairly. I can guarantee your safety.'

'No, you cannot. And you will fly where I tell you, or I will shoot Miss Bates. Move back, please.'

Yurichenko advanced, the automatic now pointed at Kyle's chest. Kyle stepped aside, and Yurichenko placed the barrel on Bates' temple. 'I mean it.'

'Shoot her and we all die.'

'I will make her suffer first, Mr Kyle.'

'2,000 feet, Kyle. I can't *stop* us going down...'

Kyle held Yurichenko's gaze. The Russian's face was impassive. He would do it.

'1,500 feet.'

'All right.' Kyle nodded. 'I've got it, Bates.' He took his place in the pilot's seat, eased the machine up. Bates wasn't wrong; it was heavy going. Down to 800 feet.

Come *on*...

The nose began to lift, slowly. *Too* slowly...

Spray coated the windscreen, wind buffeting...

Bates in the co-pilot's seat, white-knuckled, clutching her knees…

'Hold tight.' Kyle heaved back on the stick. If they were going to ditch, he'd rather ditch horizontally, give them a chance to get out.

He risked another glance at the altimeter.

850.

870.

1,000.

He breathed again, grinned shakily at Bates. He spoke over his shoulder to Yurichenko. 'How about you check Gordiovski? I don't fancy a repeat performance.'

'He's out cold,' Yurichenko said. He reached forward with a scrap of paper, numbers scrawled on it. 'These are your new co-ordinates,' Yurichenko said. 'Nothing foolish, please. I can still inflict pain; a great deal of pain.'

'You're a fun guy to travel with,' Kyle said. 'In the meantime, maybe you can tell me what's on your mind.'

Yurichenko took a seat, this time directly behind Bates. 'I will tell you.'

30

The aircraft was back at a cruising altitude of just below 3,000 feet. The skies were clear.

'I spoke of my wife, my child,' Yurichenko said.

'You did. They left you. Some disgrace or other? A frame-up, you said. And then, prison.'

'*Da,*' Yurichenko acknowledged. 'My wife and daughter are serving time in *Perm-35*. You know what this is, Mr Kyle?'

Kyle didn't; he shrugged, looked blank.

Bates helped him out. 'A *gulag*. A prison camp for dissidents.'

Yurichenko nodded. 'Correct. And for what? For what have they imprisoned a fifteen year old child?'

'Something your wife did or said would be my guess,' Kyle suggested. 'Your government don't usually need much of an excuse to bang people up, or so I've heard.'

'There was a meeting, a small gathering to discuss human rights and Ukrainian independence. Nadya attended. The meeting was raided, all attendees taken away. Those with children over thirteen were sent to Perm-35, those with children under this age were separated from them and sent to Perm-36. They have been locked up ever since.'

'How long?' Bates asked.

'Seven years.'

Kyle was concentrating on his flight plan, but it was hard not to feel some measure of sympathy. 'There are other ways you could approach this, *Kapitan*. Work with dissidents at home – or defect, create some international outrage.'

'I have tried.' Yurichenko's voice cracked with emotion. 'Now they will listen. I have Gordy by his balls, and I have the means to drive my point home.'

'You can't seriously mean to detonate the bomb in the UK,' Bates said, tight-lipped.

'I will do what I have to.' Yurichenko's grip tightened on the automatic. 'You speak of outrage. Who is outraged at the treatment of Soviet citizens, apart from their friends and families? No one! If the world paid more attention to the plight of these innocents I would not be forced to take such drastic action. But no one is listening. No one. Not the West, not my superiors, whom I begged for leniency, not the highest authorities.'

'Amnesty International?' Bates suggested.

'I am forbidden to interact with them,' Yurichenko said. 'They do what they can, but the Soviet *gulags* are impenetrable.'

'I'll talk to my bosses at MI6,' Bates said. 'We'll work something out. Together we—'

'Together is impossible.' Yurichenko interrupted Bates with a blow to the back of her seat. He placed the Makarov's barrel against her neck. 'Just follow my instructions.'

'I wouldn't expect much sympathy from MI6 if you intend to hold them to ransom,' Kyle said.

'I have information,' Yurichenko said, 'of enormous benefit to your secret service.'

'Well, you've put a price on your head,' Kyle said. 'And I hope it works out for you. Nothing personal, but if I do get the chance, I will kill you.'

'Of course.'

'Glad we understand each other. I mean, information and political ping-pong's not going to be very relevant if you turn half of Southern England into a radioactive zone, you follow? Not to mention a possible trigger for World War Three.'

'You must do as you see fit, Mr Kyle. But I will not hesitate if you threaten me. First Miss Bates, and then yourself.'

Kyle's eyes ran over the instruments. Pity there were no passenger ejector seats. 'I'm half-dead already,' Kyle told him. 'One more bullet won't make much difference to me.'

'Concentrate on your job, Mr Kyle.'

Bates had been searching in the cockpit's document pockets. She extracted a map, opened it and passed it to Kyle.

'RAF Broadway?' Kyle had the map spread on his knees. 'Abandoned in the Fifties, I recall?'

Bates was also studying the map. 'South of Swindon, middle of nowhere. Farmland. I wonder if the farmer's expecting us?'

'All is prepared,' Yurichenko said. 'Your government imagines that it has made a ... clean sweep? – of our operatives in England, but it is not so. There are always one or two who are too clever to be caught; they slip through the net.'

'Big expulsion op, a week or so ago,' Bates explained. 'Operation Foot.'

'Stanhope's been busy, then?' Kyle said.

Bates nodded. 'Oh, yes.'

'It makes no difference,' Yurichenko said. 'Everything has been prepared. Just fly.' He tapped Kyle on the shoulder.

Behind them, Gordiovski slept on.

31

Kyle let his head fall back on the headrest as the plane decelerated to taxiing speed. It hadn't been an easy landing. Crosswinds, a heavier aircraft than he was used to; they'd hit the ground hard, but the C-212 was, as far as he could tell, intact. A crash landing with a nuclear device on board wasn't something he'd wanted to dwell on, and he was grateful he'd had a lot to think about in preparation for landing. There'd been no room for mental catastrophising.

'Nicely done, Kyle.' Bates unclipped her belt.

'The hanger,' Yurichenko pointed to the edge of the overgrown airstrip. 'Over there, please.'

Kyle pointed the C-212's nose in the direction Yurichenko had indicated. As they rumbled slowly across the turf, a figure appeared by the corner of the building and raised a hand in greeting.

'I'm assuming that's not the farmer,' Kyle said.

'The area has been secured,' Yurichenko said. 'There is no farmer.'

Kyle felt Bates stiffen, and he knew why. Yurichenko had this whole thing figured out. That wasn't good news. Kyle preferred to deal with an improvising enemy; they made mistakes, not immediately perhaps, but eventually.

He brought the machine to a standstill. Weeds sprouted from the hanger's foundations, and a line of four paint-flaked windows, one cracked and three empty, the glass long gone, stared mournfully at them from a dark interior. A light rain was falling. Kyle opened the pilot's door and Bates shivered, wrapped her arms around herself.

'Welcome to sunny Blighty.' He unplugged his headset, undid his seatbelt. His legs were heavy, leaden, his ribs a band of pain across his torso.

Yurichenko was first to disembark, making straight for the man they'd seen from the runway. He was stocky, dressed in slacks and a heavy naval peacoat. Kyle and Bates watched through the open door as Yurichenko and the man conversed with much pointing and gesticulating. Eventually the man shrugged and walked away. A car engine fired somewhere nearby, the noise fading into the distance.

Yurichenko levelled the automatic at Bates. 'Bring Gordiovski inside.'

It was a struggle. Between them they managed to haul the unconscious Russian to the C-212's passenger door. Kyle wiped his brow. 'Let me look in there,' he said to Yurichenko, gesturing at the hanger. 'There might be a trolley, or a trailer. Anything to help.'

Yurichenko responded with a terse nod. Kyle left Bates in the aircraft and went into the derelict building. It smelt musty, disused, but there was also a strong tang of aero fuel. He soon realised why. Two large tanks of fuel had been deposited at the far end, provision for a new destination. By one wall an old table had been balanced on rotting legs, propped up on piles of bricks. Spread over its surface was a selection of canned food, several loaves of bread, a pallet of canned soft drinks and a stack of chocolate bars. At least they wouldn't starve.

As his eyes grew accustomed to the low light he saw what

he was looking for – an old trailer in the corner, its wheels rusted and caked with mud. He seized the handle and tugged it experimentally. The wheels groaned and squeaked but the trailer moved surprisingly easily. He wheeled it into the open.

Yurichenko was sitting on a lichen-covered staddle stone smoking a cigarette. He nodded with satisfaction. 'Take him inside. Any sign he's coming round, another shot. Understood?'

'Perfectly.'

Between them he and Bates wrestled Gordiovski onto the trolley, and dragged him into their temporary shelter. Once they were out of Yurichenko's eye-line Kyle looked at the unconscious body and then at Bates. She nodded, understanding his silent message; they would need Gordiovski before this was over.

Yurichenko appeared in the doorway and stood watching them. He stubbed his cigarette out on his heel. 'And now, Miss Bates, you will accompany me to contact your superior. Mr Kyle, you will stay here with him.' He pointed at the slumbering Gordiovski. 'If you are not here on our return, Miss Bates will die, but in any case someone will be along shortly to keep an eye on you.'

'Got that. Mind if I grab something to eat?'

Yurichenko nodded, and then gestured to Bates. 'You will bring food for us.'

Bates selected cold drinks, a loaf of bread and a few bars of chocolate. She looked at Kyle. 'See you shortly.'

'Not if I see you first,' Kyle said, unwrapping a Mars bar. Bates rewarded him with a fleeting smile on her way out, Yurichenko following close behind.

Kyle perched on the edge of the table, which creaked ominously beneath his weight, and considered the sleeping Russian on the trolley. 'Well, Gordy. What *are* we going to do with you?'

32

Bates stomped through the muddy field oblivious to the steady downpour. She was tired, hungry, and in dire need of a change of clothes and a hot bath. Yurichenko's footsteps slapped behind her, a few paces between them to allow him thinking and reaction time should she deviate from his instructions.

Truth was, she had no intention of physical violence – not yet, anyway. She just wanted to talk to Stanhope. Once that connection was made, she'd have support – remote, it was true, and unspecified, but intelligences greater than her own would be set to work to find a resolution to the problem they were about to be set.

And what a problem it was – Stanhope was going to love this.

Yes, they'd brought the asset back successfully to the UK.

Yes, they had the US warhead.

No, unfortunately they weren't in a position to bring Gordiovski in.

Why not?

Ah, yes, glad you asked, sir…

At the edge of the airstrip a rutted path led into a clearing dominated by a concrete stilted-granary; behind this, next to a green and rust-mottled Nissan hut, an open gate gave access to a thatched farmhouse. It was twilight, just after nine, but no lights were on. The building had an air of desertion – or something else.

'Keep moving.' Yurichenko prodded her in the small of the back with the pistol. She walked along the path towards the farmhouse. A line of pot plants on either side and two hanging baskets above the porch, both in bloom, spoke of recent occupation. The front door was open.

A narrow, uncarpeted hallway, a hatstand, a slim oak table on the worn surface of which stood an old-fashioned Bakelite telephone. Bates glanced down as something caught her eye. A few drops of watery blood spotted the worn floorboards and the chipped paintwork of the skirting board.

'Call them.'

Bates picked up the received and dialled a number. The call was answered immediately.

'Stanhope.'

'Jude Bates here.'

'Where the hell are you?'

'It's Yurichenko, sir. He wants you to talk to the Kremlin. He wants his wife and daughter released. When that's done, he'll play ball.'

'Bloody cheek. Who does he think—'

'Sir, he has the device, and it's armed. He's threatening to use it.'

Silence.

Bates pricked up her ears at the sound of a car engine. The peacoat man, returning?

'You have Kyle with you?'

'Yes, sir.'

'And Gordiovski?'

'Yes. In a … ah, a co-operative state.'

'Well, that's something.'

Yurichenko grabbed the receiver. 'You will provide proof that my wife and daughter have been released and escorted to the airport at Perm. You will ensure their inflight safety, and you will bring them to me. You have twenty-four hours; there will be no negotiation. In the meantime, do not attempt to approach me. You will telephone this number when it is done. The consequences if you do not comply I will leave to your imagination. I hope that is clear enough.' He returned the receiver to Bates.

'Message received, loud and clear,' Stanhope said.

'He's armed the warhead. He means it, sir.'

Another silence. Then, 'Yes. Yes, I believe he does.' Stanhope's tone was more clipped than usual. 'I'll get onto Moscow. In the meantime, sit tight. Use your initiative. You'll have friendlies in the area shortly.'

'Sir, I don't think that—'

Stanhope rang off.

'Good.' Yurichenko nodded as Bates replaced the receiver. 'Now we wait.'

Kyle finished another chocolate bar, threw the wrapper distractedly onto the earthen floor and considered his options. Gordiovski was showing no signs of regaining consciousness, but then the Russian *silovik* had been given enough sedative to fell an ox, so that was hardly surprising. One less problem to worry about.

Kyle went to the door. Night was drawing in and the rain had stopped. The silhouette of the C-212 with its doomsday cargo lay against the fading grey of the horizon like a raven guarding its territory.

What if he simply wheeled Gordiovski back to the plane and took off?

End of nuclear threat.

End of Bates.

Besides, he was low on fuel. It would take time, effort and a great deal of noise to refuel the C-212 using the stored tanks.

Second option – he could sneak after Bates and Yurichenko, wait for an opportunity to disarm the Russian.

Too risky. He daren't jeopardise Bates' situation.

But surely the reality was that as soon as she got in touch with MI6, they'd both become expendable in Yurichenko's eyes. Once she'd made that call, and Stanhope and his crew had the number, Yurichenko could detonate the bomb right here, no need for any further flying.

Yurichenko had Gordiovski for bargaining, and he had the warhead.

Kyle frowned.

No real need for Yurichenko to keep them both alive.

Not anymore.

Sure, it might not endear him to MI6, but the *Kapitan* had crossed that line already.

A shadow fell across one of the filthy windows, an indistinct shape moving slowly and carefully.

Yurichenko's peacoated friend was back.

Kyle felt his hackles rise, scanned the floor, bent and picked up a broken hoe.

Giza mode.

33

Bates sat on the arm of the sofa. The sitting room was basic, but comfortably furnished. An oak dresser, a standard lamp, a Grundig TV on a metal stand. A coffee table strewn with magazines and yesterday's Daily Express. A pair of slippers by the open hearth. A set of brass tongs, a poker, a shovel.

'What have you done with the farmer?' She sipped from her can of lemonade.

Yurichenko, sitting opposite her in a well-used armchair beneath a leaded window merely shook his head.

'This isn't the way to go, Alek.' She tapped the can with her fingernail. 'But it's not too late.'

Yurichenko gave a dismissive snort. 'Can you imagine a place like *Perm-35*, Miss Bates?' He shook his head. 'I do not think you can.'

'I do understand, you know. I'm an ex-prisoner, too.'

He snorted again. 'There are prisons, and there are prisons.'

She nodded. He was probably right. The *gulags* were infamous, and her own experiences, horrendous though they'd been, were almost certainly not comparable.

'I'm sorry your family have suffered. I really am. My people have influence. We can negotiate for their release without this—'

'You have been useful, Miss Bates.' Regret passed briefly over the *Kapitan's* face, but then it was gone.

Bates swallowed, glanced at the fireplace. 'And can still be.' She drained the lemonade. 'What's the point of saving your family if you aren't going to be around for them?'

'I will be … around,' Yurichenko smiled sadly. 'Your government will pay anything, do anything for the information I have,' he tapped his forehead, 'in here.'

'Whatever you've got, they won't liaise with a murderer.'

'Collateral damage? Isn't that what they call it, Miss Bates? I do not anticipate a problem convincing your people of your treachery – after all, I was a witness to your disposal of Mr Pearce.'

Bates said nothing.

'You see? You have no … what is it you say? No leg to stand on?

If she ducked, moved fast enough, could she roll behind the second armchair, grab the poker?

And then?

She braced herself.

Yurichenko slowly levelled the automatic, pointed it directly at her. 'As I said, I am so sorry that th—'

The farmhouse shook on its foundations and an orange glow lit the room. A second later the window blew in, sending fragments of glass zipping through the air like deadly flechettes.

Bates, already tensed and ready to move, threw herself to comparative safety behind the spare armchair, hunkered down behind it as the deadly shards studded the upholstery and shattered against the far wall. A second explosion rattled her teeth as she tried to mark Yurichenko's position but when she poked her head around the chair there was no sign of the *Kapitan.*

She grabbed the poker, ran into the hallway and out into the open air. Yurichenko was ahead of her, sprinting towards the outbuilding. Clinging to cover where he could, he skirted the granary and paused at the Nissan hut.

Poker in hand, keenly aware how ridiculous a weapon it was, she followed at a distance. There was one certainty she could hang onto: this was Kyle's doing.

Yurichenko's friend was almost at the door. Kyle had nowhere to go. He lay down, assumed the recovery position. Kept very still.

Who shoots a dead man?

Measured footsteps approached, cautious, on the alert.

Kyle held his breath.

A foot poked him in the ribs. It hurt, a lot.

Kyle lay still.

Rough hands grabbed his shirt, turned him over.

Kyle opened his eyes, swung his fist in a wide haymaker, felt it connect with flesh and bone.

With a grunt of pain, his would-be killer sprawled to Kyle's left.

Kyle twisted, got onto his haunches. The automatic was still in the guy's hand.

Kyle lunged for it, got there a fraction too late. The gun went off; he felt the bullet zing past his ear…

… and hit one of the aero fuel tanks.

Kyle turned as the first explosion ripped part of the roof away directly above the fuel dump. One tank holed, the rest about to ignite.

He gave the guy's wrist a vicious twist, heard the bone snap. The automatic fell to the floor.

He had seconds before the whole dump blew.

Gordiovski.

Kyle grabbed the trolley handle and pulled hard.

Gordiovski's arm trailed as they exited the building just as the flames reached the remaining tanks. Kyle was thrown to the ground by the explosion, and Gordiovski's trolley rolled slowly away onto the airstrip.

Kyle lay flat, covered his head as bits of roof and glass rained down. The heat was intense. He crawled after Gordiovski, hands and knees crunching on broken and burned bits of concrete and metal, eyes searching this way and that for a trace of his would-be assassin.

Vanished.

And then Bates, yelling. 'Kyle! Watch out!'

Kyle, watch out…!

A shadow, barely the ghost of a movement by the Nissan hut.

Kyle dived behind the trolley as bullets pattered around him. He counted five shots. One hit the trolley bed, and one struck the heel of his shoe and sent shock waves through his ankle. He made a decision, scrambled upright and set off in a crouching run towards the nearest cover, the C-212, hauling Gordiovski's gurney behind him.

The firing stopped.

Reloading…

Something moved near the C-212's rear ramp. The assassin. The fuel procurer, the provider of food and drink, the clearer of the way; Yurichenko's KGB contact. Or rogue agent, more likely…

Kyle reached the aircraft and let go of the trolley. Yurichenko wasn't after Gordiovski. He was still a useful asset, a prize to be negotiated for.

He narrowed his eyes. Had his assailant retrieved the automatic?

Unlikely. Not enough time between his wrist snapping and the second explosion.

The assassin wasn't coming after him. He was skulking.

On the defensive.

Kyle spared a brief thought for Bates. He had to assume she'd got away from the *Kapitan*.

Priorities, Kyle. First the gunman, then Yurichenko.

Kyle edged along the aircraft's fuselage. Apart from the C-212 itself, there was scant cover, just the burning hanger behind and the open space of the airstrip. Maybe a couple of hundred metres to the tree line.

The assassin knew it.

Kyle knew it.

Nowhere to run, buddy...

Kyle stooped, peered beneath the fuselage.

Nothing.

The ramp was up.

He paused, waited.

The slightest sound from the other side of the C-212, a soft scraping...

There was a nacelle immediately above the wheel on either side. Kyle was standing by one. There would be one opposite. Easy to get a grip, pull yourself up.

No visibility beneath the fuselage.

Kyle ducked under.

Two steps across to the opposite nacelle.

Reach up...

And grab.

Kyle's fingers came into contact with material. He took a good handful and pulled. The guy came down heavily, landing on his back like a floundering fish. His good hand was already reaching inside his jacket, mouth twisted in rage.

A spare automatic, or a knife maybe.

But Kyle had all the advantage; height, gravity, the muscle power of his leg. He stamped on the gunman's neck, hard.

Game over.

Kyle unprised the dead man's fingers and fished out the

contents of his inside pocket.

The pistol was tiny, a PSM semi-automatic. He checked the cartridge. Seven rounds left. Made sense.

Next problem: Yurichenko.

34

Bates' back was pressed against the Nissan hut's corrugated surface. She peered around the corner drainpipe just as Yurichenko snapped off a few shots in the direction of a running figure, lit up as though by a Flanders flare, propelling Gordiovski's trolley towards the C-212.

She held her breath.

And breathed again as Kyle reached the aircraft in one piece. Yurichenko was reloading. He looked up, saw her, clipped a new cartridge in place, snapped it shut with a decisive *click*.

She pulled her head back from the corner as the first round smacked against the drainpipe, the mosquito-like *ziippp* of the ricochet passing close enough to galvanise her legs into action.

Collateral damage? Isn't that what they call it, Miss Bates?

Not if she could help it. Bates took off, legs pumping, raced past the farmhouse, over a ditch, across a lane into an open field.

No good. No cover.

Stick to the lane, find cover behind the hedgerow, the trees. Anywhere.

She stopped by a young oak, leaned on the trunk, panting.

Had he spotted her?

Crack!

Bark flew; a splinter gashing her forehead.

She took off again, lungs heaving, the beginnings of a stitch tightening a band around her midriff.

She stopped, bent double.

Another shot, wide this time. Had he lost her?

There was a gap in the hedgerow, a kind of tunnel in among the foliage. Protecting her eyes with one hand she squeezed inside, stumbled on with branches and leaves flicking her face.

She had to stop, just for thirty seconds.

She squatted, breathing hard, struggling to suppress the noise she was making, her desperate gasps for air.

'Miss Bates.'

Too close. She froze.

'Miss Bates. I need you by that telephone.'

Liar.

'When they have complied with my request, I will hand myself in.'

Bates gulped air.

The voice went on, reasonable, persuasive. 'You have been most helpful.'

She weighed her options. To her left the green tunnel narrowed, becoming too dense to negotiate, certainly without giving her position away. Turning right, however, would take her straight to Yurichenko.

'I have changed my mind. Please accept my apologies for causing alarm.'

No options.

How many rounds had he used? Three? She couldn't rely on Yurichenko running out of ammunition, then. A bad bet.

So. The direct approach.

She'd dropped the poker somewhere between the Nissan

and here, but the earth at her feet was studded with flint. She bent, selected a fist-sized chunk. One end was razor sharp, the other blunt enough to grip.

So be it.

'I have put the gun away, Miss Bates. May we return to the house? It would be unfortunate to miss the call from your colleagues. Your co-operation would be much appreciated.'

She hefted the flint.

'I mean you no harm.'

Where was he? She inched forward. There. Between a thin birch, silver in the moonlight, and an oak, just at the edge of the field, Yurichenko was a deeper smudge of darkness in the oak's shadow.

Another two paces, leaves crunching softly beneath her feet.

'I hear you. Come out, please.'

She slipped through a gap in the hedgerow, this time on the tunnel's opposite side, skirting round so she could circle in from behind. Leaves gave way to ploughed earth. She was in the field. She ghosted over puddles, roots, a sliver of half-buried barbed wire...

Now she was close, two or three yards, maybe. Yurichenko was motionless, waiting, watching.

He'd lost track of her.

She moved towards him, made a fist around the flint.

At the last second he sensed her presence, spun around, his arm coming up.

Bates smashed the automatic aside with a sweeping blow. Yurichenko cursed and clutched his injured hand as the gun tumbled to the ground. Bates followed her first strike with a second but this time the Russian was prepared. He shimmied to one side and the rock caught him on the shoulder, not on his head as she had intended.

Yurichenko jabbed his fist at her face. She ducked, drove

forward with all her weight and knocked him to the ground. The flint segment was still in her hand; she raised it high to finish the job, but realised that Yurichenko's eyes were shut and he wasn't moving.

She knelt over him, legs astride his prone body, grabbed his lapels and lifted his head. It flopped back as she released him. There was blood in his hair. The ground beneath them was strewn with rocks, projecting through the earth like broken teeth; one of them had knocked him cold.

Bates stood up, panting, looking for the gun. She found it nestled between two exposed roots. Yurichenko was groaning now, semi-conscious. She bent, checked his pockets. A bar of chocolate. And something else...

She withdrew a small device similar to a transistor radio, held it up for inspection. Two external buttons, an indicator light. Bates' forehead creased as she examined it.

No idea...

She pocketed the device and thought about what to do with Yurichenko. He wasn't going anywhere in a hurry, that was for sure.

Find Kyle. Call Stanhope. And between them get Yurichenko back to the farmhouse.

It seemed a reasonable plan.

Bates set off the way she had come, grateful for the pale light of the waxing moon.

35

Kyle checked the living room. A discarded chocolate bar, an empty can of lemonade.

No Bates.

He returned to the hall and jumped as the phone rang. He picked up the receiver.

A familiar voice. 'Hello? Bates?'

'Guess again.'

'Ah, Mr Kyle. Good to hear from you.' Stanhope sounded buoyant. 'You have Yurichenko with you?'

'Not exactly.'

Stanhope ignored that. 'Been in touch with Moscow. Fair to say they're not over the moon about his proposition.'

'Half of England will be over the moon if they don't change their minds.'

'Point taken, but look, Yurichenko's no fool. He knows that setting a nuclear device off would be tantamount to starting World War Three. He won't go that far.'

'You don't think?'

'Where is he? Put him on.'

'I'd love to, but he's busy trying to kill Bates, so if it's all the same to you I'll sign off for a bit. And for God's sake don't send in the cavalry. That'll only inflame the situation, no pun intended.'

A pause. 'All right. You'd better handle this, Kyle. What about Gordiovski? Safe and secure?'

Kyle glanced up as Gordiovski shambled into the hallway. The Russian's eyes had looked murderous enough onboard the C-212 but right now, from where Kyle was standing, they were incandescent with rage.

The two men looked at each other for a long moment. Kyle dropped the receiver as Gordiovski hurled himself at him, fists flailing like twin pistons.

The first swing missed but the follow through struck Kyle on the shoulder, fair and square. It was like being hit by a bulldozer. A seismic shock ran through his upper body, spine and ribcage.

He went down, and struggled to rise. He was on all fours, his head ringing, nauseous. His shoulder felt dislocated.

Maybe Gordiovski wouldn't come at him again. The Russian had put him down with a single punch. That was enough, wasn't it?

But Gordiovski was just getting warmed up. His boot connected hard with Kyle's thigh and then twice more in succession, torso and shoulder. Kyle curled himself into a ball. Each blow was a hammer of agony. A mantra began to play in Kyle's head like a needle stuck in a groove.

Get up. He's going to kill you…

In his mind, Kyle imagined a rugby field, a loose scrummage. Players piling on top of him. His one focus, the ball.

Get the ball. Don't stay here. You can't stay here.

Supporters were cheering from the touchline, but he was hurt too badly. How could he continue?

In his mind he saw a face in the crowd. Indistinct at first, the features gradually swam into focus.

Rebecca.

His ex-fiancée.

Her lips were moving; she was speaking quietly, but he could hear each word with crystal clarity.

Come on, Kyle. You're out there to win, remember?

Gordiovski's leg came swinging in again, but this time Kyle rolled and it passed harmlessly by. The cost was more pain, but that wasn't going to get better any time soon. Gordiovski was off balance and Kyle launched himself off the floor, hit the Russian in the midriff, gave gravity a chance to help out.

Gordiovski staggered against the wall with a reverberating crash, dislodging a mirror above the telephone table which shattered as it dropped to the floor. Another haymaker was coming; Kyle ducked under it, scooped up a shard of glass, brandished it.

The Russian hesitated. His face bisected into a wide grin.

Kyle jabbed, and Gordiovski moved back, an agile move for a recently tranquillised man.

Kyle slashed, aiming for the trunk-like fold of Gordiovski's neck. Gordiovski's fist smashed Kyle arm aside, and he let go of the glass dagger. Blood dripped freely from his cut fingers. Lacking any other options, Kyle put his head down and charged like a bull. He hit Gordiovski's muscle wall with everything he had. It was like slamming against an oak tree. The Russian didn't move.

Kyle felt hands like mechanical diggers encircle his biceps. He was lifted bodily from the floor, legs flailing.

One hand moved to his throat and Kyle was lifted high, suspended in mid air.

Gordiovski held him there, as though examining a lab specimen.

'Leave him!'

Bates's voice came to Kyle from a far-off place. His vision was fogging.

'Last warning!'

Kyle hardly heard the gunshot. He found himself on the floor, lying amid broken glass.

'Back off!'

Bates…

Another shot, louder this time.

Gordiovski roared.

Kyle raised his head in time to see the Russian wrestle Bates to the ground. Blood was pooling on the floorboards from Gordiovski's wounded legs.

And then Bates was down, and Gordiovski was back on his feet.

Kyle managed to sit up, prop himself against the wall. His strength was gone.

He could only watch as Gordiovski tore strips from his shirt to tourniquet his bleeding legs. He seemed otherwise unaffected by Bates' bullets.

Bates…

She wasn't moving.

Gordiovski completed his improvised first aid and turned his attention to Bates' prone body. He fished in her pockets and let out a grunt of triumph, lifted his head to the night sky. He stood quite still for almost a minute, as though gathering his courage to make a difficult decision.

Kyle found his voice. 'Now what, Gordiovski?' He was surprised to hear himself sounding close to normal. His throat felt like it had been sawn in two.

Gordiovski turned and looked directly at him. In his meaty hands he held what looked like a small transmitter.

'Now?' Gordiovski grinned. 'Now I turn your South England into a nuclear wasteland.'

36

'Pointless.' Kyle shook his head wearily. 'What will you achieve? Notoriety?'

Gordiovski shrugged. 'This is an American bomb, salvaged and detonated by a minor terrorist group. Officially, it has nothing to do with me, nothing to do with Russia.'

'You're aware that your Kremlin buddies have thrown you to the wolves?' Kyle flexed the muscles in his legs; maybe they would support him, maybe not. Only one way to find out; grimacing with the effort, he used the table edge to pull himself upright.

Gordiovski looked unconcerned, so Kyle kept talking. 'They knew you'd be up for this. They played to your ego. The only place you're heading for is an MI6 debrief – without your cronies to protect you. Then everything you spill gets passed back to your KGB boss man. End of your private kingdom. They'll take you all down.'

Gordiovski held the transmitter's metallic case lightly in one hand, Bates' automatic in the other. He shot Kyle a humourless grin.

'I do not intend to keep the rendezvous with your MI6, Mr Kyle. And when I return home it will be to a heroes welcome. As your expression goes, my stock will have risen considerably. My superiors will have no choice but to to acknowledge my achievement. Not publicly, of course; no, publicly we will condemn this terrorist group along with the rest of the world. But once the investigation is complete and the origins of the bomb come to light, we will very much enjoy observing the deterioration of your country's relationship with America.'

'You have more faith in the Kremlin than I do.'

Gordiovski shrugged. 'No. I do not. What I do have is power. Connections. They cannot touch me, Mr Kyle, not in my home country. Your correspondents in Moscow will be able to observe and report my rise to ultimate power at first hand.'

Kyle shook his head. 'You're deluded. No wonder they want to get shot of you.'

Behind Gordiovski, Bates stirred. Her leg moved a fraction, then was still. Kyle willed her to stay put.

'Think what you will,' Gordiovski said, dipping into his coat pocket and pulling out two pairs of handcuffs. His trousers were stained with blood, but the wounds didn't seem to be troubling him; in and out through the fleshy part of the leg, in all probability. Lucky for him, unlucky for them.

The Russian bent, dragged Bates into the hallway, clipped her wrist to Kyle's. 'Get her up. Walk.'

Kyle supported Bates as best he could as they exited the farmhouse, Gordiovski's lumbering steps close behind. Their heads close, Bates whispered in his ear.

'Yurichenko. He's injured.'

'One less to worry about,' Kyle said. 'What about you?'

'Head hurts, but I'm OK.'

'I can relate.'

The outbuilding was still burning; the roof was gone and dirty smoke was still rising into the darkness. Gordiovski jabbed the automatic into the small of Kyle's back. 'The plane.

Move.'

'Really? We're low on fuel. You can't—'

'How far?'

'How far what?'

'Range. How far can we fly?'

Kyle thought about it. Not far; maybe a hundred miles, a hundred and fifty max. He told Gordiovski.

'It is enough.'

The body of the other gunman was still lying where Kyle had left it. Gordiovski ignored the corpse and prompted them inside.

Kyle flexed his wrists. 'I can't fly cuffed.'

Gordiovski unlocked him. 'Fly. To London. And you, sit.'

Bates sat next to Kyle and Gordiovski cuffed her to the seat base.

'What about Yurichenko?' Kyle busied himself with pre flight checks.

'What do I care?' Gordiovski said. 'MI6 can do what they wish with him.'

Bates was pushing something towards his feet. A medical bag.

Kyle leaned forward, flicked a switch, dipped his hand in the bag. His fingers closed around a slim, plastic barrel. He withdrew the hypodermic, slipped it under his knee. He only managed a quick glance but it had looked half-loaded, at least. Enough to put Gordiovski out.

If he got the chance.

Deep in the C-212's underbelly, a rumbling noise began to vibrate through the aeroplane followed almost immediately by the pungent smell of aero fuel.

Gordiovski started forward, grabbed Kyle by the shoulder. 'What are you doing?'

Kyle sat back, slapped his thighs. 'Damn. Sorry. Dumped the fuel. My mistake – poor design, though; all these switches look the same.'

The blow arrived earlier than Kyle had expected. Even so, he managed to move his head fractionally to the left so that Gordiovski's fist connected with the base of his neck and not his skull. Then the Russian's meaty hands were around his neck and he was being shaken like a puppet. His vision blurred.

'*Stop*! You'll kill him!'

Bates' protests fell on deaf ears. Kyle felt himself blacking out, but then the pressure was abruptly released. He sucked in air and his hands went to his bruised windpipe.

'You come with me. Insurance. Get up.'

Dazed, Kyle did as he was told. Gordiovski took out a set of keys, opened the pilot exit, deployed the steps and shoved Kyle out of the aeroplane.

'You can't leave her here.' Kyle turned to look into the aircraft. Bates shook her head. 'Just do what he says, Kyle.'

Gordiovski shoved him in the back. 'Walk.'

They went past the smoking remains of the hanger, through the farmhouse yard and into the lane. Gordiovski produced a set of keys and led them to Yurichenko's late assistant's car, Kyle supposed. 'Get in.'

Gordiovski was limping. Kyle looked him up and down. 'You need medical attention – those wounds might look superficial, but you've lost a lot of blood.'

'My problem. Get in.'

Kyle shrugged. 'I'm not driving?'

Gordiovski silently held the passenger door open.

Kyle got in, and Gordiovski cuffed his left hand to the seat. Leaving his right hand free. A mistake.

Gordiovski crammed himself into the driver's seat, gunned the engine and threw the car into gear.

'You're going to trigger the bomb remotely?' Kyle clucked his tongue. 'In a Wiltshire field? Hardly the impact you were looking for.'

'It will be sufficient.' Gordiovski squinted through the windscreen as rain began to patter on the glass.

'Really? You think your Moscow pals will be impressed? "Hey, I blew up a field in the UK."'

'The blast radius will be ten miles.' Gordiovski ignored Kyle's jibe. 'The incident will be reported world wide. This whole area will be a no man's land for years to come. That is an impact.'

An image of Bates swam into Kyle's mind, trapped in the C-212, inches away from the bomb, swam into Kyle's mind. He shut it out; the transmitter was key. Disable that, and Gordiovski's teeth would be pulled. The Russian had placed the device under his seat before setting off.

'And we're going where, exactly?'

'Away from the blast zone. Lucky for you, eh?'

The sky was lightening with the first touch of dawn. The car sped along the narrow Wiltshire lanes, trees and hedgerows flicking past on either side – trees and hedgerows that would be vaporised within the hour, along with a certain someone who, he was now able to admit, had risen to a position of key importance in his life.

No choice, Kyle.

Only one thing would now make the difference.

The transmitter.

37

Gordiovski took a corner fast. Kyle wondered whether Stanhope might be planning on sending support, despite his earlier instruction not to; there was nothing now to stop MI6 moving in on the plane, although they couldn't know that. If they could get to it, though, maybe they could disable the bomb's receiver before Gordiovski pressed the trigger.

He just had to send them the all clear.

Somehow.

But Gordiovski wasn't going to allow phone calls home, so that was a non-starter.

The Russian was focused on the road ahead, intent on escaping the blast zone. But how far would he drive? That depended on the megatonnage of the bomb, and Kyle had no clue. Ten miles? Forty? The transmitter would have a limited range, but Gordiovski and Yurichenko would no doubt have factored that in … when they'd been working cooperatively.

'Hands where I can see them,' Gordiovski said, with a sidelong glance.

Kyle rattled his left hand. 'Can't move it much further. Sorry.'

'The other.'

Kyle slid his right hand across to his right knee. The

hypodermic was in his left hand pocket.

The wrong one.

The lane narrowed again. Woods on either side. Trees didn't move. If he went for Gordiovski now they'd go off the road and hit a solid trunk. They probably wouldn't survive, not at this speed.

But then there would be no one to trigger the transmitter signal. Which meant no explosion.

Which meant Bates would live.

Kyle watched the countryside flash past, feeling as though his life were retreating into itself, into a recursive series of rapidly changing images. So he would die.

So what?

He'd lived with the prospect for so long now. Did it really matter?

But something had definitely changed. He was increasingly aware that he'd moved on from the "nothing to live for" bleakness of the weeks and months following the abortive stakeout.

Why?

Simple.

Her name was Jude Bates.

The sense of loss and hopelessness he'd felt after her apparent betrayal came back to him with vivid intensity. He hadn't wanted to believe she could turn traitor so easily – more than that, he hadn't wanted to believe that she could set him up and leave him to the mercy of two ruthless rogue Russian militants. That wasn't the Bates he had come to know. His relief as she whispered those redeeming words to him in the plane had been off the scale.

He wouldn't let her die. Not now.

Never.

Kyle considered the best line of approach.

Go for the weak spot – always.

He stole a glance at the bloodstains on Gordiovski's trousers. The guy's pain threshold was more than impressive; Bates' bullets looked to have hit Gordiovski's left thigh and the fleshy part beneath his right knee. Kyle weighed up which injury was likely the more painful.

The thigh. It was also the nearest option.

Gordiovski slowed as a T junction loomed, and Kyle took his opportunity. He reached over, grabbed the Russian by the thigh and squeezed as hard as he could.

Gordiovski howled and let go of the wheel. The car swerved, ploughed through a fence and kept going. Kyle saw a glint of brightness fifty metres ahead, closing fast. He hoped it wasn't what he thought it might be.

He let go of Gordiovski's leg and seized the Russian's wrist, the hand holding the automatic, just as the big man's finger squeezed the trigger. The gun went off, punched a hole in the roof. Kyle pivoted his elbow into Gordiovski's nose and felt cartilage crunch, but the Russian's grip on the automatic held fast. Kyle's strength was ebbing; little by little Gordiovski was reducing the angle, the automatic's muzzle creeping closer and closer towards Kyle's head.

Kyle changed tack, made a grab for the handbrake and pulled hard. The car slewed and skidded. Gordiovski was propelled forward and smashed himself in the face with the automatic. The gun fell into the space between the seats and Kyle flicked it into his footwell. He fumbled in his left pocket for the hypodermic. The car was still moving; it tilted forward, nose down. Water cascaded over the bonnet and windscreen.

The glint of brightness; a lake.

There was a brief floating sensation before the weight of the vehicle began to drag it down. Kyle gave up on the hypodermic; even if he managed to extract it with one hand he still had to remove the needle guard.

Gordiovski was shouldering the driver's door, but the weight of water held it shut. The driver's window was half open, sky still visible. Gordiovski tossed the transmitter through the gap as Kyle hooked his fingers into Gordiovski's trouser pocket, felt for his keys and fished them out. Water was pouring through Gordiovski's window as the Russian repeatedly heaved his weight against the door. Kyle fumbled with the keys as the water level reached his waist. He tried the first.

Wrong.

And the next.

Wrong again.

The third slid into the lock without resistance. Kyle turned the key and shook off the cuffs. Gordiovski's strength had forced his door open enough to push his bulk through. The pressure equalised, the door stayed open, but the car was sinking rapidly. Kyle took a breath, stuck his head in the flooded footwell and groped for the automatic.

There.

The car completed its slow journey to the bottom of the lake and came to rest with a bump. Kyle hauled himself to the driver's door and squeezed through.

He kicked out for the surface, a grey, shimmering ceiling far above him.

38

Kyle broke the surface in time to see Gordiovski dragging himself onto the lakeside mud like an oversized amphibian. He trod water but was dismayed to discover that he'd dropped the automatic somewhere between the surface and the lake bottom.

Great...

The Russian was struggling to find his feet; it seemed his injuries were finally hampering his movement. Kyle watched the Russian fall once, twice before he could persuade his legs to support him. Finally, he heaved himself clear of the mudbank, and in a shambling crouch began to hunt for the transmitter.

Kyle starting swimming. The water was freezing, sapping what little remained of his energy, and his clothes were heavy and getting heavier with each exhausted stroke. Gordiovski was still fully focused on his search as Kyle dragged himself from the water and lay on his back gasping like a stranded fish. His head and heart were pounding like a drum and he had never felt so cold. He lifted his chin in time to see Gordiovski retrieve something from a clump of willow and hold it aloft, before letting his head flop back onto his outstretched arms. *Damn...*

But he had no time for lying around; Gordiovski wasn't hanging about. He was already heading for the road.

Kyle made himself crawl until he reached a grassy area that looked to be more or less negotiable on foot, got himself onto all fours and then, on shaking legs, gingerly tested his balance. He fell heavily on his way up the slope to the fence, jarring his ribs and telegraphing pain into his shoulder, neck and head. He rolled onto his back, groaning; it would be so much easier just to stay where he was, close his eyes, wait for someone to find him, take him somewhere warm where he could forget everything.

He struggled to his feet and resumed his climb up the bank. Lungs heaving, he reached the fence, used a broken post to pull himself up the final slippery gradient. He ducked under the shattered wood onto the verge, looked to his left and then to the right.

Gordiovski had flagged down a car, a Ford Cortina.

The driver didn't look to be too happy, which was hardly surprising, given Gordiovski's wet and dishevelled appearance. Kyle could see the driver, a middle-aged businessman, through the rear windscreen. He was shaking his head – a definite no. The engine revved and Gordiovski tried to grab the door handle, but the driver wasn't having any of it. The car sped off, leaving Gordiovski off-balance and staggering at the roadside.

Kyle cast about him for some weapon. A hefty branch, or … anything. Then he remembered the hypodermic. He felt in his pocket.

Thank God…

As Kyle removed the needle guard and checked the contents, Gordiovski broke into a limping trot away from the road, heading for a nearby wood.

Shivering like a man with the ague, Kyle followed.

The woodland gradually got thicker, until Kyle was

following Gordiovski through a denser proliferation of trees and shrubs. Somewhere nearby a robin trilled. Kyle crunched steadily through an undergrowth of mulchy leaves and rotting branches. He'd lost sight of Gordiovski, but the Russian couldn't be far ahead. By now, Kyle reasoned, he must have lost a lot more blood.

Which would weaken him considerably.

Just enough to administer the sedative.

Not a big ask.

A fox dashed across a clearing ahead, startling him.

But something had startled the fox.

There.

Gordiovski was propped against the first of a pair of stocky alders, seeded in all probability by the same gust of wind. On his lap lay the small box, his spade-like hand resting gently on its simple controls.

Kyle approached slowly, tucked the hypo into the palm of his hand. 'We're still too close. You'll die with the rest of us.'

Gordiovski took his time replying. Maybe he was close to passing out.

Too much to hope for?

Eventually the Russian made a *comme-ci, comme-ça* gesture. 'No matter.'

Kyle was just a couple of metres away. 'So you've changed your mind? What happened to the hero's welcome? Your inevitable rise to power in the Motherland.'

Gordiovski shrugged. 'There are others who can take my place.'

Kyle kept his eyes fixed on the transmitter. A red light was blinking on its cold surface. It looked intact, operational.

'And it's worth it? The destruction of so many lives?'

Gordiovski waved his hand dismissively. 'You think you are untouchable, you English. You live on your island and dream that the glory days of empire are still with you. You side with the Americans against us. You send spies to Moscow masquerading as journalists. By your actions, you reveal yourselves as our enemy.'

'But you won't find us detonating a nuclear bomb near Moscow. There's a difference between a potential enemy and a real one.'

'Words, words.' Gordiovski shut his eyes but quickly reopened them.

Kyle's heart missed a beat along with his momentary opportunity. He took a half step closer.

'Give it up. We'll treat you fairly. We don't send opponents of our culture to labour camps.'

'Perhaps not.' Gordiovski smiled. 'But I have come this far. Yuri could not stop me. You will not stop me.'

Gordiovski's finger lifted a fraction.

Kyle was rooted to the spot. He couldn't stop Gordiovski. He had failed.

The finger came down.

Click...

Kyle closed his eyes.

39

'Camila? Are you there?'

Arianna tutted as she examined the contents of her daughter's jeans pocket. She was used to finding all manner of things in such places. Camila's bedroom was always full of surprises – shells, discarded trinkets found on the beach, odd and unidentifiable items from the harbour, a snakeskin, and once, a whole lizard skeleton, bleached white by the sun.

They were staying at Arianna's sister's house in Vera. Francisco had wanted to put some distance between themselves and what had happened at home. He wanted his family to forget, to heal. Their house was for sale; they would move nearer to Cristina, maybe even to Vera or its outskirts.

It was nice here. Camila loved the beach and her cousin, Jacinta, and there would be work for Francisco. For her part, Arianna was happy so long as her family were happy. But there was no doubt in her mind that the events of the past weeks had taken their toll. Camila's nightmares, Francisco's unsettled mood, her own memories and fears, had all followed them.

She wondered what had happened to the woman, Jude Bates, and her English friend. She hoped they were all right, that they had somehow escaped the clutches of *los Russos*. But that was no longer her concern. The bad things were over, finished. It was her job to restore normality, to be the best mother and wife she could be.

'Camila? *Que es Esto?*'

Arianna examined the tiny item in her hand. It looked like an electrical component of some sort, but where had Camila found it?

'She is playing.' Francisco was at her side. 'With Jacinta, in the garden.' He slipped his arm around her waist. 'But let me see.'

She gave the object to her husband.

'Hm. *Es un condensador, tal vez?*' He shrugged.

Arianna didn't know what *un condensador* was. It didn't matter anyway. There was laundry to wash, a meal to prepare. She kissed her husband as he put the tiny object in his pocket. 'Go.' She smiled. 'Go and look at your beautiful, clever daughter.'

'She is like her mother, no?' Francisco returned his wife's smile as she shooed him out of the room.

40

Kyle opened his eyes.

He looked up. The sky was still there. A breeze riffled the treetops. The robin alighted on a nearby bush and eyed him beadily.

Gordiovski's eyes were closed, his head slumped on his chest.

Kyle got down on his haunches and prised the transmitter from the Russian's sausage-like fingers. Gingerly, he unclipped the back panel. A set of batteries nestled in one corner of the densely packed circuitry. Kyle removed them with trembling hands. He had no idea what had happened, but something had caused the transmission to fail.

He knelt by Gordiovski's still body and allowed exhaustion to sweep over him.

Kyle lost track of time. He could have been lying on the woodland floor an hour, a day, a month even. He felt himself slipping in and out of consciousness, of reality. Sometimes he was underwater, sometimes running through a dense forest. He was trapped in the stinking hold of a fishing boat, and then locked in an airless room onboard a Russian support ship. The more he wanted to open his eyes, the harder it seemed to be; so he drifted in and out, unable to surface.

'Hello? Are you all right?'

Someone was shaking him by the shoulder.

'Goodness me. Whatever's happened to your friend?' The voice was cultured. Bates would have used the word "posh".

Kyle blinked. A grey-haired woman in a Barber and a bobble hat was bending over him, her rouged cheeks spotted with rain.

'I need to get back,' Kyle managed.

'Get back where, for heaven's sake?' the woman said. 'You need a hospital, young man, that's what you both need, by the look of it. My friend's already called an ambulance. You're lucky we spotted you – we don't usually come this way. Was it a wild dog or something? Or a giant cat, perhaps? One hears of such things, you know.'

The sound of a siren drifted through the woods from the direction of the road. 'Do you live nearby?' he asked her. 'Could you contact someone for me?'

'Your wife? What's her number?'

'Not my wife. His name is Stanhope.'

'Stanhope, Stanhope? Stanhope who?'

'He works for the Security Services. MI6. Just call 100 and ask for him. They'll put you through.'

'Security? *Security*? Well, I—'

'Thank you. I would very much appreciate it.' Kyle rose slowly to his feet in time to see a second woman emerge from the direction of the road accompanied by two uniformed and burly ambulance men.

The woman harrumphed. 'Aha. Here's Marjorie now. MI6, you say? Well, I never. What shall I say to this Stanhope?'

Kyle thought for a moment. 'Just tell him that World War Three has been postponed.'

41

Once Kyle was content that the police presence at Gordiovski's bedside was sufficiently aware of what they were dealing with he left them to it, refusing any medical treatment himself. Nothing much to be done for bruised ribs, cuts and contusions. He did, however, concede to a pack of strong painkillers.

Kyle's upper-class rescuer had made the call as he had requested, and Stanhope had duly called in the cavalry. He had also arranged a car, so Kyle took the lift to the hospital's ground floor and headed out to the car park. An ordinary looking man in a plain shirt and slacks greeted him with a perfunctory nod, handed him a set of keys and indicated a white Morris Marina.

'I was hoping for a Lotus,' Kyle said as he took them.

The man's expression remained deadpan.

'Have a nice day yourself,' Kyle said.

Once out of the hospital car park, he guided the Marina onto the main road and mentally retraced the route he had taken with Gordiovski. It wasn't far, twenty minutes, maybe.

As he drove, he thought about Yurichenko. The man had been desperate. Had he survived? Had Stanhope contacted Moscow as the *Kapitan* had requested? And what would be the outcome?

He passed the lake and shivered. A knot of police blue and white Morris Minors and an AA recovery vehicle were busy dredging the lake for the remains of the sunken car.

Kyle put his foot down.

Ten minutes later he was stopped by a roadblock.

He identified himself at the cordon and was waved through. He parked the car by the farmhouse and got out. Two men carrying a stretcher were negotiating the farmhouse path. On top of the stretcher lay a zippered body bag. Kyle waited for them to pass, exchanged a grim nod, and made his way past the Nissan hut in the direction of the airstrip.

The C-212 still held centre stage. The rear ramp was open and a cluster of overalled technicians were moving purposefully to and fro along the length of its stubby fuselage. A tractor and trailer were parked behind the ramp. The pilot's door was open, the steps down.

Bates was sitting on the top step, chewing on an unlit cigarette. She nodded as he approached.

'They'll kill you, those things,' Kyle said.

'It's not on fire, look.' Bates held the cigarette up for inspection.

'And neither are you, I'm pleased to see.'

'You look like crap. I can't wait to hear the story,' Bates said, climbing down. 'But it'll have to wait. Stanhope wants to see you.'

'Where?'

'In the farmhouse.'

'I just saw—'

Bates nodded. 'The farmer. He was in the cellar. Wife's away at relatives.' She shrugged.

They walked together.

'How's the head?'

Kyle grunted. 'Around a three. Which, all things

considered, isn't bad.'

'See? You're more robust than you thought.'

'My ribs are the problem.'

'They'll heal.'

'Sympathy noted. How's Yurichenko?'

'Ah…'

They were walking up the path to the farmhouse door. 'What's that supposed to mean?' Kyle stopped, caught her arm.

'He's gone, Kyle.'

'What do you mean, gone?'

Bates stuffed her hands in her pockets. 'He was out cold. There was blood. I went to find you. I thought it was safe.' She moved pebbles around with the tip of her shoe.

'Not your fault,' Kyle said. 'I'd have probably done the same.'

'Stanhope's not happy.'

'So we'll face the music together.'

They went in. Stanhope was sitting at a corner bureau in the lounge. A china teapot, cup and saucer were placed next to the telephone, which had been moved from the hallway to the bureau. It was ringing. Stanhope picked it up, waved them in, pointed to the sofa.

'Stanhope.'

They watched him listen to the caller. He frowned. 'No. Out of the question.' The handset went back into its cradle with a bang.

Kyle felt like a recalcitrant schoolboy summoned into the headmaster's presence. He waited for Stanhope to speak.

'So,' Stanhope folded his arms. 'One half-dead, one missing.'

There was a brief, awkward silence.

'But no nuclear explosion – sir.' Bates said. 'Faulty transmitter. A missing component, according to the boffins.'

Stanhope considered this. 'An odd oversight, but lucky for you, mm?' He scratched an imaginary itch on his stubbled chin. It looked like he hadn't slept in a while. 'That aside, what I was rather hoping for was the safe delivery of two high-ranking Russians, preferably in one piece.'

'Gordiovski will recover,' Kyle said. 'The man's constitution is something else.'

'And *Kapitan* Yurichenko?' Stanhope's eyebrow elevated a centimetre.

'Can't have gone far,' Kyle said. 'Injured, disoriented—'

'No joy so far with the police search.' Stanhope cleared his throat, raised the teacup to his lips and peered over the rim. 'So I suggest you get a move on.' He replaced the teacup carefully in its saucer. 'I'll press on with the politics, if that's all right with you?'

Stanhope's manner suggested a certain urgency. Bates was already on her feet.

Kyle could have sat on the sofa for a month. He allowed his head to rest momentarily on the faded antimacassar before bullying himself to his feet.

Stanhope dismissed them with a curt nod and a tight-lipped smile. 'Don't take too long, will you?'

42

'He's a barrel of laughs.'

'He's under a lot of pressure.' Bates led them to the lane. 'Follow me. I'll show you where I left him.'

They waited at the gate for a squad of army personnel to pass by on their way to the C-212.

'They still haven't unloaded it.' Kyle said. 'Why the delay?'

'Making sure it's safe to move?' Bates suggested. 'At the end of the day we still don't know what Yurichenko was working on inside the mechanism.'

As they watched, the military personnel took up their pre-allocated places around the aircraft – two at the front, two in the centre, two at the rear.

'The Americans are going to love this,' Kyle said.

'They might not even get to hear about it,' Bates said, hands on hips. 'It'll be disarmed and squirrelled away in some covert underground bunker. Too much of a political hot potato to make a song and dance over.'

Kyle nodded. 'Sounds about right.'

They continued along the lane. Kyle said, 'If you were Yurichenko, where would you go?'

Bates considered this as they retraced her nocturnal route into the foliage at the field's perimeter. 'He's a desperate man.

In a strange country, cut off from any military assistance – or any KGB assistance, come to that. I don't think there's a single agent left in the UK after the recent sweep.' She ducked under an overhanging bough and Kyle followed. 'Here. This is where he was.'

Kyle bent and examined the spot.

'He banged his head – on a rock. I think it was this one.' Bates squatted. 'Yep. See? Blood.'

'OK. So, unless he was carried off by a wild animal he can't have been injured that badly.'

Bates stood up. Her face was smudged with grime and her hair was awry, but her movements were assured and graceful. He loved the way her nose wrinkled when she was thinking.

'What are you staring at?'

'Nothing.' He went to the edge of the green tunnel and looked into the field. A few sheep, a crow preening itself on a distant tree stump. He took a breath. 'I'd lie low. Stick around until nightfall. The only leverage Yurichenko has now is inside that plane.'

Bates joined him. The crow took off, sailed into the dusk with a raucous cawing. 'I think you're right. He's near. I can feel it.'

Kyle pursed his lips. 'The boys in blue didn't find anyone – and they've turned the area upside down.'

She made a disparaging noise in her throat. 'So?'

Kyle grunted an acknowledgment. 'Point taken.'

Bates did the wrinkling thing again. 'The C-212 has an armed guard. How's he going to get inside without being spotted?'

'How would you?'

Bates frowned, her tongue protruding slightly as she turned over the possibilities. 'Impersonation,' she said after a while. 'Or take a hostage.'

'Sounds about right. Better stick around then, yes?'

Darkness was falling rapidly as they backtracked towards the farmhouse. Two searchlights placed at the airstrip's edge illuminated the bulky shape of the plane, the armed guards' shadows chequering the fuselage, breaking up its silhouette.

'Plan?' Bates leaned on the Nissan. The farmhouse interior lights were on. Stanhope and his politics. Two policemen bookended the front door. Both looked bored out of their minds.

'Wait and watch?' Kyle suggested.

'Let's get this done, Kyle. He's here somewhere. You want to wait till he's got the advantage? I don't.'

'Fair point. I'll start in here.' Kyle went to the rusted door of the Nissan.

'Hang on.' Bates followed him. 'Together is better. And you'll need this.' She handed him a stubby-nosed automatic. 'Walther PPK/S. Seven rounds.'

Kyle took it. 'Thanks.'

'Don't kill him. Stanhope will *not* be happy.'

'Well, we can't have that.'

'I'll cover you.' Bates checked the magazine of her own PPK, slotted it back into place.

Kyle pushed the Nissan door open. The carcass of a rusted tractor squatted in the centre space like a knocked-out tank. The air was tinged with the smell of rotting straw, perished rubber. Kyle did one circuit and came out. 'Nothing.'

'OK. Where else?'

'Somewhere he can lie low, keep an eye on the plane. Wait for an opportunity.'

'Around the perimeter of the strip?'

'The police have it covered.'

'Worth another look, then.'

He didn't argue. They started by the embers of the hanger. All that was left was a pile of smoking ash and blackened bars of metal – pieces of the original frame. They covered the ground in twenty minutes; every ditch, tree stump, and a half-sunken World War Two air raid shelter. Not a trace.

They made their way back to the farmhouse. One of the uniformed police raised a hand in acknowledgment. He was on his own; his buddy was probably on a comfort break or sneaking a quick fag.

'Too quiet, don't you think?' Kyle scanned the airstrip for the umpteenth time.

'Yep.'

'How long after Gordiovski drove off before you were found?'

Bates thought about it. 'A couple of hours, maybe. Police got here first. Then Stanhope and co. The boffins arrived much later – just after first light.'

'So there was time for Yurichenko to recover, make his way back here. Hide away.'

'Yes. But we've checked everywhere.'

'Except the farmhouse.'

'It's been scoured. They found the farmer in the basement. No one else.'

Kyle looked the building up and down. 'Big place. Who's to say they found all the potential hiding places?'

'Maybe we were wrong. Maybe he's miles away by now.'

As Bates spoke, the farmhouse door opened. The policeman dropped to his knees and pitched forward, face-planted into the gravel.

Stanhope appeared in the doorframe, and behind him, Yurichenko.

Holding a gun to Stanhope's head.

43

'On the other hand,' Kyle said, 'maybe not.'

'Disperse them, please, Mr Kyle.' Yurichenko's voice floated across the space between them. 'Weapons empty, on the grass where I can see them. Both of you, then the guards.'

Kyle placed his PPK on the ground. Bates did the same.

'Kick them away, please.'

They did as Yurichenko commanded.

Yurichenko began a slow, awkward walk towards them, Stanhope dragging his heels to hinder their progress. 'I can't see them moving, Mr Kyle.'

Bates said, 'Better do it.'

Kyle trotted to the CASA, found the senior officer. 'Name's Kyle – working for Stanhope.' He offered his hand, which was gripped in a firm handshake.

'James Routledge – Captain, Royal Engineers.'

Kyle briefly and apologetically explained.

Routledge scowled, barked an order. With threats and curses, the detail laid their rifles down and Kyle led them back to the quadrangle.

'Hands on heads, please.' Yurichenko had reached the end of the path. He moved sideways, maintaining a good distance, keeping a close watch on the disgruntled troops.

'Keep going, that's good. Mr Kyle, you will join the squad inside the house and arrange a field telephone to be brought to the aircraft – within the hour. Mr Stanhope will then resume his conversation with Moscow. Hands where I can see them, Miss Bates. You will come with us. Walk in front, please.' To Kyle he said, 'I will kill him if I have to, Mr Kyle. And Miss Bates.'

'Same orders apply,' Stanhope said evenly. 'Safe delivery.'

Kyle clenched his fists as Bates, Yurichenko, and Stanhope walked slowly across the airstrip and boarded the aircraft.

He went to talk to one of the searchlight operators at the airfields edge, a lance corporal in a camouflage jacket.'Keep the searchlights trained on both exits,' Kyle told him.

'No problem.'

He headed back, picked up his PPK on the way. Inside the farmhouse he sought out Routledge.

'Can you organise a field telephone?'

'Of course.'

Kyle was thinking furiously. Yurichenko had planned and executed his move to perfection. Now he had two hostages – and the bomb.

The phone rang. Kyle picked up the receiver.

A clipped male voice said, 'Century House here. Stanhope, please.'

'Ah,' Kyle said. 'He's not available at present, I'm afraid. Who am I speaking to?'

'Century House. Use your loaf, man. Where's Stanhope? Put him on, would you?'

Kyle was tempted to dissemble but the caller didn't sound as though they would tolerate obfuscation. He came clean.

There was a heavy silence at the other end. 'I see. Well, we have the wife and daughter standing by. That should help the situation.'

'Here? In the UK?' Kyle was amazed. 'That was damn

quick.'

'Our Russian friends are very keen on this Gordiovski debrief. They're happy – no, wrong word, content is better – to let Yurichenko walk if that's the price to ensure it happens.'

Kyle said, 'We already have Gordiovski in custody. Yurichenko's no threat to the debrief now.'

'True – but it was a different story twelve hours ago, Mr Kyle, was it not?'

'Yes, yes, I suppose. What do you want me to do?'

'I'll send them directly to you. I suggest you inform Yurichenko that we've complied with his wishes and that – if he wants the big reunion to happen *sine lacrimis* – he should release Mr Stanhope and your colleague lickety-split.'

'Will do. What's the ETA?'

A pause.

'Should have them with you by midnight at the latest.'

'Right.'

Kyle wondered how to sign off, but the caller had already hung up.

44

Kyle walked slowly towards the C-212, hands held aloft. He was a few metres distant when the cabin door opened.

'That's close enough, Mr Kyle.'

'I'm unarmed, and I come bearing good news.'

Kyle saw a shape move across one of the windows. Bates or Stanhope. He was surprised that Yurichenko hadn't restrained them, but it made him feel slightly better to see signs of life.

'What news?'

'Your family are in transit. They were released according to your wishes and took off from Bolshoye Savino Airport late this afternoon.'

'Are you telling me the truth, Mr Kyle?'

'Why wouldn't I? I suggest you release Mr Stanhope and Miss Bates, and then join us in the farmhouse. Better to receive your family in a civilised manner than invite them to join you in a hostage situation, don't you think?'

Silence. The searchlights tracked back and forth along the fuselage, then returned to focus on the cabin door where Yurichenko was taking care not to expose himself to sniper fire.

'Come on, *Kapitan*. You've got what you asked for. You're

not going to endear yourself to my superiors if you carry this on any longer.'

'I want proof.'

'I've just been speaking to Mr Stanhope's colleagues. They've arranged transport for your wife and daughter who are on their way here as we speak. I give you my word.'

Silence.

'This isn't a surrender, Yurichenko. It's an acceptance of favourable terms.'

'I asked for a telephone line.'

Kyle shook his head. 'No need.'

'Then I will wait. When my family arrives, you will escort them to me here. If all is well, then I will lay down my weapon. Not before.'

'You're jeopardising your position, *Kapitan*.'

'These are *my* terms.'

Kyle sighed. Exhaustion had shortened his already reduced fuse to a stub. He wanted to charge the plane, disarm Yurichenko, wrap this up. Instead he took a second to calm himself. 'Very well. Your call.'

He trudged back to the farmhouse and the enquiring faces of the Royal Engineer squad. 'A waiting game,' he told them. 'He's not budging until he's seen his wife and daughter in the flesh.'

Routledge looked at his watch, and then at one of his men. 'Righto. Rogers, put the kettle on, would you?'

They waited. An hour passed; the engineers drank tea, played cards, joked, smoked. Eventually Kyle set down his empty mug and looked at his watch for the umpteenth time.

Eleven forty. Almost time.

He looked at Routledge. 'Police roadblock still up and running?'

Routledge nodded. 'Yep. Two armed, one plod.'

Kyle grunted. There was only one way in. What was he worried about?

'I'll take a walk, check them out.'

'As you wish,' Routledge said. 'We're not going anywhere.'

Outside the air was still, the atmosphere calm. Hard to believe there was a desperate man with two hostages and an A-bomb just a few metres from where he stood. It was surreal. He shut the farmhouse gate behind him and walked across the quadrangle to the lane. An owl hooted from somewhere deep in the copse. Kyle kept walking.

Two police cars came in sight, parked obliquely across the narrow lane. Mobile lights had been erected, flooding the area around the vehicles in brilliant white. Kyle hailed one of the uniformed shapes standing by the left hand-car. He identified himself and the policeman relaxed, lowered his gun.

'No sign?' Kyle asked him.

'Not yet.' The officer's jacket identified him as Wilson D.

The second officer sauntered over. His ID read Phillips A. Like his colleague, he held his Heckler and Koch rifle barrel down, trigger finger extended across the guard. Kyle introduced himself. 'Where's the constable?'

Wilson jerked his thumb towards the police car parked on the right. 'Having a twenty minute kip.'

'Lucky guy.' Kyle forced a smile. He could sleep for a week. No, make that two.

'All quiet. No trouble expected, right?' Phillips said.

'Hopefully not,' Kyle agreed.

He left them to their duties and made his way back to the farm.

Routledge looked up as he came in. Kyle shook his head. 'As the grave.'

He accepted another mug of tea, went to the farmhouse

window and looked out. He could only see the tip of the aircraft from where he was standing. He fretted about Bates, hoped she wouldn't do anything rash. What was the time? He consulted the mantel clock. Just after twelve. Where were they?

As if on cue, the smooth rumble of a car engine brought them all to their feet. Kyle was first to the door. A black Mercedes Benz pulled up, engine purring, and a tall man in a dark suit got out, did a quick 360 degree survey, and then opened the back door furthest from the house.

A woman emerged from the vehicle and stood to one side, arms folded across her chest as a second passenger joined her. A girl, maybe in her early twenties. They both looked bewildered, lost. They were both bone-thin, their clothing grey and colourless. The woman bent and retrieved a coat from the interior of the Mercedes and hung it around the younger girl's slender shoulders. Then the tall man led them up the path towards the house.

'Kyle?' The tall man looked to be in his forties. His features were nondescript, neither handsome not plain, a prerequisite, no doubt, for his assigned duties.

The two men shook hands, and the two women were ushered inside.

Kyle turned his attention to the new arrivals. They looked pale, shell-shocked. He wished he could speak even basic Russian, but instead was forced to rely on slow, simple English. 'Hello. My name is Kyle. Your husband is on board the aircraft outside. I will take you to him. What are your names?'

'Nadya Yurichenkova.' The older woman eyed the soldiers with deep suspicion. 'And my daughter, Irina.'

Kyle attempted a reassuring smile. 'It is perfectly safe,' he said. 'Please. Follow me.'

45

'Give old sleeping beauty a nudge, would you?' Wilson said.

Phillips walked over to the Morris, tapped on the side window. No response. He tapped again, peered through the glass.

A tiny trickle of blood ran down the side of the uniform's cheek and gathered on his chin. The head flopped forward onto the steering wheel. Phillips spun around, his finger now firmly in contact with the trigger of his Heckler and Koch. Wilson was on the ground, not moving, his arm twisted at an impossible angle under his body.

Phillips' training kicked in; he dropped to a crouch to lower his profile, began to traverse the rifle. He'd made five or six degrees of his intended three sixty when the sniper's round drilled a neat hole in his temple and the tarmac rushed up to meet him.

Kyle's father had once told him that the longest walk a man could take was from the cricket pavilion to the wicket. But Kyle was a rugby man, not a cricketer, and he doubted whether his father had ever experienced a walk like this one.

He led the two women across the dewy grass towards the aircraft, feeling as though he was traversing a minefield. The weight of unease he had felt during his walk to and from the checkpoint had not lifted with the arrival of the Mercedes; it made his bones heavy and his feet clumsy, as though he was negotiating a mire. The women were holding hands, their chins tilted expectantly towards the aircraft's cabin door.

Just a few more yards…

The cabin door opened a crack. Kyle glanced back at the house, fretting that one or more of Routledge's squad might yet be trigger happy in spite of their orders to stand down, but all was quiet.

The cabin door opened and Yurichenko appeared in the full beam of the searchlight. He lowered the steps, climbed swiftly down. He stood stock still for a moment, as though unable to believe what his eyes were telling him. He spoke just one word:

'*Nadya.*'

Routledge gave up trying to make conversation with the Mercedes driver, drained his mug and went outside for air. A movement in the corner of the quadrangle caught his eye. He stiffened, then relaxed. One of the ARU cops. He raised a hand and the man returned a brief salute. Good to know they were taking their job seriously, patrolling rather than waiting statically by the roadblock. One on the block, one to roam. Made sense.

He went back inside. The men were getting more and more restless, the banter degrading into jokes at each other's expense as time went on. Still, he told himself, this particular *non*-assignment would soon be over and he could harry them back to barracks for what remained of the night. Who knew where they'd be assigned in the morning?

He slumped in an armchair, picked up a farming magazine, thumbed through the pages. The spill from the searchlights gave him just enough light to read by. The only other illumination in the room was a standard lamp in the corner, a single twenty watt bulb. Whatever else the farmer had been in life, he'd certainly been frugal. Routledge flicked over a page.

And the searchlights went out.

The first bullet passed close enough for Kyle to feel the movement of air.

'*Get down! Flat!*'

The daughter, Irina, was already lying prone. Kyle rugby-tackled Nadya to the ground. He lay across her as the second round whickered past and hit the fuselage with a loud *smack*.

Bates was at the cabin door, just her head and arm visible. She had a handgun. Yurichenko's?

Get down, Bates, get down...

She snapped off a few shots in the direction of the Nissan.

One of the searchlights came back on, the beam swinging towards them. Routledge's voice, yelling. 'It's all right, he's running! He's in the lane!'

But it wasn't all right. It was far from all right. The yellow beam illuminated the scene. Yurichenko was lying face down, arms spreadeagled. Nadya crawled towards him, tried to turn him over. Kyle saw the blood-soaked shirt and groaned.

Irina, crying, pulling at her mother's arm. 'No. No. Noooo! *Papochka, Papochka*'

Nadya, cradling her husband's head, turned and looked at him.

Kyle knew that he would never forget that look.

Bates joined him. She squeezed his hand. 'Not your fault, Kyle. None of this is on you.'

They stood back a short distance, giving the two women some space as they pressed themselves against Yurichenko's motionless body. The sound of their weeping filled Kyle's head like an *a cappella* requiem.

46

'You lied.' Kyle hadn't rehearsed his opener, but that pretty much summed things up. 'All bullshit. A bioweapon? Really?'

Stanhope registered no surprise at the question. 'A necessary evasion, for reasons with which you are now familiar. Shall we move on?'

'So,' Bates said quickly. 'Operation Foot missed a few.'

'Missed *one*. That was enough,' Kyle muttered. He traced a line with his forefinger in a light covering of dust on Stanhope's desk. It seemed an age since he had first sat here, been coerced into the Spanish trip. Everything was identical – the inkstand, the painting hanging over the empty fireplace, the mahogany drinks cabinet, Stanhope's expressionless face… Identical, and yet everything had changed.

Stanhope sighed. 'Unfortunate. For us, for Yurichenko, for his family…'

'*Unfortunate?*' Kyle leaned over Stanhope's desk. 'She watched her husband die. She was two feet away. And the daughter – I mean, can you imagine…?' He trailed off.

'Look, I do understand. But what *you* must understand, Mr

Kyle, is that this sort of thing is par for the course. We win some, we lose some. And in this particular case, we have a big win in Gordiovski. The Russians are champing at the bit for his intel.' Stanhope was doing his best to sound sympathetic and positive but it wasn't cutting much ice with Kyle.

'Is he out of danger?'

Stanhope shook his head. 'Out of ICU and in a secure side ward across the road at the Westminster. Should be fit enough for interrogation in a week or so. Earlier if I had my way.' He went on before Kyle could interrupt again. 'Furthermore, in many ways we do not blame Moscow for taking matters into their own hands regarding Yurichenko. In their eyes he was a traitor, pure and simple. The man was a loose cannon. He might have initiated World War Three.'

'We should have protected him! For God's sake, we had an ARU, an army squad…'

'And two MI6 officers,' Stanhope said pointedly.

Kyle fell silent. What was the point? Nadya's face haunted his dreams. Probably always would.

'I told them it was safe,' he said quietly. 'They trusted me.'

'You weren't to know, Kyle,' Bates said. 'None of us were.'

'We bloody should have known. Any intel on the shooter?'

Stanhope shook his head. 'Sadly not. He'd have been commissioned by the KGB before Nadya and her daughter even got on the plane.'

'You make it sound inevitable.'

'Not inevitable. Just highly likely.'

'What about the Americans, sir?' Bates said. 'Have we told them anything yet?'

Stanhope clasped his hands in front of him on the desk. 'Not yet. I imagine we'll wait until we're in a position which requires us to exert a little leverage on our friends across the pond. Favours offered, favours granted, and so on. No need to tell them about our little collaboration with Moscow, not at all – it might be a Cold War for them in the here and now, but it's all a bit lukewarm for us, post-Foot, to be honest. We will tell the US we've found their missing bomb, but all in good time.' He shrugged. 'Kudos in the bank. In the meantime, the warhead is safely tucked away in one of our repositories. No harm done.'

'What are Moscow offering in return for Gordiovski's intel?' Kyle asked.

'There is a long-standing ... ah, guest of the KGB whom we're anxious to repatriate,' Stanhope said. 'Negotiations still ongoing, but this will help considerably.'

'Well that's great to hear.' Kyle could think of nothing else to say.

'Will that be all, sir?' Bates asked.

'For now.' Stanhope produced one of his oily smiles. 'But don't stray too far.' He looked at Kyle. 'Either of you.'

'Wouldn't dream of it.' Kyle got up.

'Wouldn't dream of it, *sir*.' Stanhope's eyebrow twitched.

Kyle shook his head. 'Contract's ended. Formalities are irrelevant.' He headed for the door. He needed air.

Outside, the pavements were slick with rain. Traffic roared past in a constant stream. 'I don't suppose you brought an umbrella?' Bates said.

'Do I look like an umbrella carrier to you?' Kyle buttoned his jacket.

She laughed. 'Any plans for the afternoon?' She slipped her arm through his as they began to walk in the direction of the bridge.

'Not really.' Kyle looked at his watch. 'Pubs are still open.'

'And I suppose you know a nice, cosy one nearby?'

'Of course. Just around the corner from Big Ben. You'll like it.'

'You think?' Bates said, as the swollen waters of the

Thames rushed beneath them and a bus sent a deluge of water across the pavement. 'I don't suppose that constitutes straying far, so why not?'

They walked on, arm in arm, heads bent against the downpour.

47

The pub was busy. Lunchtime service, predominantly of the liquid variety, was in full swing. MPs brushed shoulders at the heaving bar with bankers, journalists and civil servants, while huddled knots of tourists crammed themselves into dark corners, jammed against the beer-stained wood panelling, straining their voices above the constant babble of conversation to reassure each other that, yes, they were having a great time.

'Nice place.' Bates wrinkled her nose.

'Best beer in the area, trust me.' Kyle pushed through the physical wall of tobacco smoke towards the bar and Bates clung to his jacket tails.

'I might not want beer. I might want something lighter. Lager, maybe.'

'Pedant. You're having beer.' Kyle looked over his shoulder, knowing that the reward of Bates' grin would be waiting. He wasn't disappointed.

Kyle used his height and voice to maximum advantage and they were soon heading to a recently vacated corner table.

Bates offered him a cigarette, which he declined. 'Maybe there's something in those health warnings after all,' he shrugged, sipping from his beer glass.

'Am I hearing this right?' Bates drew her chair closer. 'Cameron Kyle takes health warning seriously?'

He smiled. 'Progress?'

'I'll drink to that.'

They clinked glasses.

'What d'you think will happen with Nadya and her daughter?' Kyle said. 'Surely Stanhope won't send them back?'

Bates shook her head. 'I very much doubt it. They'll be given a safe house, new identities. Not that Moscow will be too interested – not now.'

Kyle thought about that.

Bates studied his expression. 'You're thinking about it again. You can't blame yourself, Kyle.'

'Then who?'

'Circumstance.'

He shook his head. 'No. We should have had it covered.'

'There was an ARU checkpoint. If any single party is to blame, it's the police. They should have allocated a bigger team. Been more vigilant.'

'Cutbacks?'

She clucked her tongue. 'No doubt.'

'It was a screw up. The whole thing.'

'They have Gordiovski. That's what Moscow wanted. That's what Stanhope wanted.'

'Even so.' Kyle rubbed his temple. The area that Yurichenko had elbowed – just above his ear – was giving him cause for concern, although he hadn't mentioned it to Bates. It wasn't like a regular headache, maybe nothing to do with the bullet fragment.

'You OK?'

'Fine. Just thinking.'

Bates took a pull from her pint, smacked her lips. 'This

isn't half-bad, you know.'

'Told you. Best in the area.'

She tapped her cigarette on the pack, thought better of it, put it back. 'So. The million dollar question.'

'Being?'

'Are you staying with us?'

'Oh, it's *us* now is it? That's rum, coming from a double agent.'

'Let's get this straight. I am *not* a double agent.' Her face coloured.

'I'm teasing.'

'It's not funny, Kyle.'

'Are you going to tell me what happened? You had me worried for a few hours.'

She examined the dregs of her beer glass. 'Only if you buy me another. That'll loosen my tongue.'

'Deal.' Kyle stood up.

And froze. He couldn't feel his feet.

His head was swimming. He put out his hand to steady himself, grasped at the air.

'*Kyle?*'

Her voice was sucked into a vacuum as the room receded in a kaleidoscope of colour. He was on the floor, the smell of ale spillages and ground cigarette ash in his nostrils. His head was pounding in a series of slow, arhythmic thumps.

He was sick.

'*Kyle!*'

A black tunnel ahead. He welcomed it. Inside, there would be no more pain.

Bates paced the corridor at the Westminster Hospital. The smell made her nauseous, sick with trepidation. The polished floors, the anonymous masked and gowned figures scurrying silently to and fro, eyes fixed firmly on their next task – all conspired to spike her anxiety levels. The waft of antiseptic and stale, funnelled air from the wards and toilets. The waiting rooms, the functional benches deployed at random; inanimate, static stations, indifferent to the living tragedies being played out on their scored plastic seats. The children, not understanding the adults' anxieties, hovering by Cadbury's chocolate machines, badgering their relatives for two pence pieces.

And to her right, the twin swing doors leading directly into the neuro theatre. Each time they parted her heart missed another beat.

He'd been in there three hours and still nothing.

'You all right, love?' A kindly-looking woman walked past holding two plastic cups of dispensed tea. 'It's the waiting that gets to you, isn't it?' She patted Bates' arm. 'It'll be fine, you'll see.' She cocked her head towards the closed doors. 'They know what they're doing in there. We just 'ave to trust 'em, eh?'

Bates smiled weakly, dabbed perspiration from her brow with a crumpled tissue she found in her pocket – the one she'd used to wipe beer rings off the pub table before they'd sat down.

'Think about all the nice things you've done together,' the woman suggested. 'That's what I do. The time will soon pass.' She offered Bates a sympathetic smile, turned the corner and was gone

Bates sat down.

The nice things.

Bullets.

Betrayals.

Beatings.

Bombs.

Maybe I'll stop there...

She stared at the wall clock, watched the minute hand

track slowly, slowly, slowly around its grimy face. A moth had got stuck under the transparent facing, and had coated the number eight with powdery detritus from its wings before it died so that the numeral now looked like a zero. She wondered if the minute hand would disturb the illusion, but the moth looked like it had been there a long time. Six o'clock, seven o'clock, zero …

Zero hour…

She lowered her head.

All you can do is wait.

Another five minutes laboured by. She counted the seconds.

Wait.

She lifted her head.

The end of the corridor gave onto a staircase, and from beyond the fire doors she could hear raised voices. Some patient with a grudge? The noise was incongruous, grating amid the hospital's habitually hushed tones.

Louder. More voices. A scream.

She went quickly to the top of the stairwell. The hospital's main entrance was just below, and she could see a small crowd gathered at the revolving doors, pushing and shoving as they all tried to exit at the same time. More screams.

Panic.

She clattered down the stairs, searching high and low for a possible cause of the exodus. Fire? She couldn't smell smoke. No alarm.

At the bottom of the stairs she grabbed a nurse as she ran past.

'What's happening?'

The woman looked at her with glazed eyes. 'Secure prisoner. Escaped. Killed a policeman. I saw it. It was *horrible.*'

'Has anyone called the—?'

But the woman tore herself away, squeezed herself through the revolving doors and was gone.

The lobby was clearing fast. Bates took up a position by the exit and waited. Patients and staff members pushed past her in ones and twos, but no one paid her any attention; all were intent on getting out. The hospital's main artery, the primary corridor, opened to her left like a wide throat. It was empty.

No.

There was someone.

A tall, shambling figure in a tattered hospital gown. Shambling, but moving fast.

Bates' heart missed a beat. She scanned the reception desk, the floor, the walls. There must be something she could use—

A fire extinguisher? She grabbed it, but it wouldn't release. She heaved again.

She felt him behind her.

Turned.

Backed away.

They made eye contact, Gordiovski's glinting with pleasure at his good fortune. He advanced slowly, savouring the serendipity of the moment. He held a scalpel in each hand, one bloody, the other pristine.

She had no words. She held up her hands, palms towards him.

And then he was on her, caught her by the neck, swung his free arm into her side, pushed her away like a rag doll.

She fell, banged her head on the linoleum. Her midriff was numb and wet. She heard the door revolve, felt a waft of petrol-laced air from the car park outside.

She was lying in a lake, a lake of red.

Night drew in.

48

Kyle knew the light was there. It was a band of brightness just above his forehead, like a halo. He wanted it to go away, but it wouldn't.

What did it mean?

He considered this for a while. There was no hurry.

He was thinking. Therefore he must be alive. Or maybe thought went on anyway after death.

Were his eyes open? He wasn't sure.

He issued a command to his brain. Or maybe his soul?

His eyes opened. It was intolerably bright.

He shut them again.

Maybe he slept then, for a while.

When he became aware of himself once more, he repeated the process. This time, the brightness didn't hurt quite so much. He was able to make out its source; a ceiling light above him. A yellow strip light. Cheap, definitely not cheerful. Hospital budget.

No strip lights in Heaven. Or the other place, presumably.

Therefore, I am alive.

Pleased with this logic, he slept again.

When he awoke, he found himself wondering at his reaction.

Pleased? Why pleased?

You're the man with no reason to live, remember?

And then he remembered. He remembered it all. Spain, the Russians. Bates, in his hotel room, in Francisco's house. On the Russian ship. In the C-212. On the steps, with an unlit cigarette.

Bates.

He smiled.

Bates in the pub, reluctantly sipping her ale. The grin as she grudgingly conceded that she liked it.

'This isn't half-bad, you know.'

Bates.

Kyle tried to raise his arm. He wondered if he was in a ward, a side room, in ICU?

He managed to touch his head. His fingers brushed against linen.

Bandage.

The effort was too great. He let his arm drop.

It didn't matter now, anyway.

He was alive.

Surprise, surprise.

Bates would be happy.

They'd both be happy.

Kyle took a deep, laboured breath. The doctors wouldn't allow visitors. Not yet.

But they would, in time.

And he knew who'd be first in the queue.

He allowed himself another smile, imagining her eyes, her grin, the way she always looked at him.

Special.

His special Bates.

Cameron Kyle returns in *A Fragile Peace* ... read excerpt below ...

'You're late.' The woman held the door open for the newcomer.

Gordiovski looked up. 'Ah, my favourite sniper. Sit down, my friend. Make yourself comfortable. Drink?' He held up a bottle.

'*Nyet.*' The man declined both offers, choosing instead to remain standing in the centre of the sparsely furnished room. Behind him, the woman shut the door.

'Your loss.' Gordiovski shrugged, held up his glass. 'Finest quality.' He winked at the woman. 'My friend here knows her vodka.'

'What do you want, Gordiovski?' The man's tone was flat, guarded. Gordiovski understood; he'd probably guessed what was coming. 'I have a little job for you, comrade. Good for you to sit. I think you will listen better, hm?'

The woman folded her arms and went to the window. Outside the traffic was thinning as the morning rush hour drew to a close. A bus rumbled to a halt at the nearby bus stop and a motorcycle slalomed past it with an angry burst of power.

'A job? The man sneered. 'I do not work for you. I work for the state.' He glared at the woman.

'Come, comrade.' The woman spoke up. 'We are united in our loyalties, are we not?'

The man ignored her. 'You are a *pariah*, Gordiovski. An outcast. Why do you think they want you here?' He extended his forefinger. 'They want to draw your teeth. And they will.'

The woman came forward. She was wearing a tight-fitting,

sleeveless vest and her arms were tattooed and muscular. Gordiovski made a small negative signal and she withdrew.

'You have a comfortable position in the UK, comrade, do you not?' Gordiovski said conversationally. 'A few jobs here and there, some big, some small; Moscow asks you because you are good at what you do, mm? You are what they call a "results" man. They can rely on you, Sergei. They ask, and it is done.' He tilted his head. 'Poor Yuri – he didn't have a chance, did he?'

'Do not tell me you would not have killed him too, if he had got in your way.'

'Maybe. But you are the expert, Sergei.' Gordiovski leaned forward and joined his meaty hands together. 'How are your charming mother and sister? I hear they are well supported.'

Sergei narrowed his eyes. 'Touch either of them, and I will kill you myself.'

Gordiovski shrugged again. 'But by then they will already be dead, Sergei, so...'

Sergei's face darkened. Moscow will not tolerate—'

'Moscow will not know anything about it, my dear Sergei.' Gordiovski smiled. 'Will they, Mira?'

The woman shook her head.

'I cannot work for you,' Sergei bristled. 'If they find out that—'

Gordiovski raised his hands in a soothing gesture. 'Not work! No, no. A simple instruction to your usual friendly contact, that is all I require, Sergei.'

'What do you want?'

'An address.'

Sergei lifted his chin. 'Who?'

'An old friend, a family member. His name was Vasily Borodin. Whatever his name is now, I would like to know. And I would like to know where he is living. You can do that for me, can't you, Sergei?'

Sergei sighed. 'This is all I will do. Whatever happens to you afterwards ... I cannot be responsible.'

'I hope that is not a threat, dear Sergei.'

Sergei said nothing.

'Of course.' Gordiovski set his glass down with a thump. 'I do not want any interference from third parties. We understand each other other, Sergei?'

Sergei glared at the reclining Gordiovski. 'Forty-eight hours. I will bring the address to you.'

'Thank you, comrade.' Gordiovski raised his glass. 'We will be waiting.'

Morozov peered through the café window. Rain was ricocheting off the pavement like a hail of bullets and the glass was misting up, making it difficult to identify passers by, but when Sergei's stocky frame came into view she had no trouble identifying her contact. She waited as he shook off his raincoat and closed the door behind him against the downpour.

The café was sparsely populated; mid-afternoon, just after lunch hour, was a good time to conduct business. Office workers had returned to their desks, manual labourers were once again bent at their tasks. Apart from Morozov herself, there were only two customers – a woman in her late sixties sipping tea from a mug, and an old man with a dog slowly working his way through a cheese and tomato sandwich as the dog looked hopefully up at its master. Behind the counter, the owner bustled about with a dishcloth, wiping surfaces, refreshing the glass-fronted cabinet with sandwiches, pastries and savouries whistling atonally along with the radio. This was always maintained at an unnecessarily loud volume, which suited Morozov and the nature of the conversations she was likely to conduct on the premises.

She sipped her coffee while Sergei ordered a drink, paid

the proprietor and eventually sat down opposite her, raising one eyebrow in an unspoken question.

She kept it brief. 'I need a name and an address.'

Sergei said nothing.

'You are still in touch with your friend, I trust?'

The assassin drained his teacup, made an expression of distaste and replaced it in its chipped saucer. 'Yes.'

She leaned in, close enough to smell his aftershave. Sergei always dressed well and liked to think of himself as attractive to women. This she knew about the man sitting opposite her – and much more besides. She knew him to be ruthlessly efficient, uncompromising, tenacious, loyal to his masters in Moscow. He was persuasive, patient, persistent and deadly accurate with his weapon of choice, the SVD Dragunov semi-automatic marksman's rifle. 'The name is Vasily Borodin.'

Was it her imagination or had there been a slight flinch, the brief appearance of a twitch along Sergei's jawline? Unusual for this man to show any reaction or emotion. She studied his face, the deep set eyes, the horizontal line of his full lips, the two shallow creases in the thin flesh of his forehead, but his expression remained neutral. 'You have heard of him, Sergei?'

He shook his head. '*Nyet.*'

'Are you sure?'

'Why do you ask?' The deep set eyes bored into hers.

She held his gaze. 'For a moment, I thought you recognised the name. That is all.'

His expression was unreadable. 'By when?'

She took a deep breath. 'As soon as you can. By midday tomorrow is preferable.'

'The usual place?'

She nodded. 'The usual place.'

[to be continued – A Fragile Peace will be available from 12th December 2025]

Enjoyed this book?

A Fragile Peace is available now!

Why not try the *DCI Brendan Moran* series from the same author?

Black December

DCI Brendan Moran, world-weary veteran of 1970s Ireland, is recuperating from a near fatal car crash when a murder is reported at Charnford Abbey.

The abbot and his monks are strangely uncooperative, but when a visitor from the Vatican arrives and an ancient relic goes missing the truth behind Charnford's pact of silence threatens to expose not only the abbey's haunted secrets but also the spirits of Moran's own troubled past . . .

Black December is an atmospheric crime thriller that will keep you on the edge of your seat until the stunning climax. This is the first in the DCI Brendan Moran crime series, one of the new breed of top UK Detectives.

'...gripping, with a really intriguing plot.'

Creatures of Dust

An undercover detective goes missing and the body of a young man is found mutilated in a shop doorway. Is there a connection? Returning to work after a short convalescence, DCI Brendan Moran's suspicions are aroused when a senior officer insists on freezing Moran out and handling the investigation himself.

A second murder convinces Moran that a serial killer is on the loose but with only a few days to prove his point the disgruntled DCI can't afford to waste time. As temperatures hit the high twenties, tempers fray, and the investigation founders Moran finds himself coming back to the same question again and again: can he still trust his own judgement, or is he leading his team up a blind alley?

'...non-stop action and convoluted twists. Another brilliant read in the Brendan Moran series...'

Death Walks Behind You

DCI Brendan Moran's last minute break in the West Country proves anything but restful as he becomes embroiled in the mysterious disappearance of an American tourist. Does the village harbour some dark and dreadful secret? The brooding presence of the old manor house and the dysfunctional de Courcy family may hold the answer but Moran soon finds that the residents of Cernham have a rather unorthodox approach to the problem of dealing with outsiders...

...a pleasure to read – gripped from start to finish...'

The Irish Detective - digital box set

The first omnibus edition of the popular DCI Brendan Moran crime series. Contents includes the first, second and third in series, plus an exclusive CWA shortlisted short story 'Safe As Houses'...

Silent As The Dead

A call from an old friend whose wife has vanished from their home in Co.Kerry prompts DCI Brendan Moran to return to his Irish roots. The Gardai have drawn a blank; can Moran succeed where they have failed?

Moran's investigation leads him to a loner known locally as the Islander, who reveals that the woman's disappearance is connected to a diehard paramilitary with plans to hit a high profile target in the UK. Time is running out. Can Moran enlist the Islander's help, or does he have to face his deadliest foe alone?

'Superb storyline with plenty of twists and turns...'

Gone Too Soon

Moran is called to a burial in a local cemetery. But this is no ordinary interment; the body of a young woman, Michelle LaCroix, a rising star in the music world, is still warm, the grave unmarked. A recording reveals the reason for her suicide. Or does it?

Why would a young, successful singer take her own life? To unlock the answer, Moran must steer a course through his darkest investigation yet, as the clues lead to one shocking discovery after another...

'...endlessly twisty – an explosive finish...'

The Enemy Inside

DCI Brendan Moran's morning is interrupted when a suicidal ex-soldier threatens to jump from a multi-storey car park ...

Moran soon regrets getting involved when an unexpected visitor turns up on his doorstep to confront him with what appears to be damning evidence of past misconduct. Can the Irish Detective clear his name, or must he come clean and face the consequences? One thing seems certain: by the time the night is over, his reputation may not be the only casualty...

'...a cracking, fast-paced thriller.'

When Stars Grow Dark

A fatal road traffic collision uncovers a bizarre murder when it transpires that an elderly passenger in one of the vehicles was dead before the accident. All indications point to the work of a serial killer – but with little forensic evidence, how can DCI Brendan Moran and his team run the killer to ground?

To add to Moran's problems, an unexpected discovery prompts the Irish Detective to undertake a dangerous and unscheduled journey to Rotterdam where he believes his former friend and MI5 agent, Samantha Grant, is being held.

Can Moran succeed in his rescue mission whilst juggling the heavy demands of his most perplexing murder investigation to date? *When Stars Grow Dark* is number seven in the popular DCI Brendan Moran crime series

'*...another brilliant outing for the DCI. No red herrings, page fillers or unnecessary characters, just gripping story leading to an unexpected ending...*'

The Cold Light of Death

July, 1976 – Thames Valley, UK. Long, scorching days of blue skies, water shortages, and record temperatures. A newly promoted Detective-Sergeant is tasked with investigating the murder of a local shop owner – an investigation that goes tragically wrong...

Fast-forward forty-five years to 2021, when a chance discovery exposes a grim secret that forces a reexamination of the circumstances surrounding the ill-fated murder inquiry.

DCI Brendan Moran is assigned this coldest of cases, and it soon becomes apparent that he is dealing with a cold and calculating criminal mind. Can Moran and his team piece together the events of that long forgotten summer and unmask the killer before history repeats itself?

'A most satisfying read, with a plot zooming back to the mid 70s. As usual, wonderfully evocative. The entire series is a must for any crime fiction fan'

Closer to the Dead

A new cold case for DCI Brendan Moran coincides with the unexpected reappearance of a dangerous adversary.

As Moran grapples with an ever-changing work culture and begins to get to grips with the forty-year old murder of a young RAF aircraftswoman, an unexpected complication arises in his personal life that threatens to sabotage a promising relationship before it even begins. Could his new friend really be involved in the shady financial dealings of a cold case murder victim?

With this uncertainty playing on his mind, Moran throws himself into the new investigation, but as he digs deeper it becomes clear that the original case was sloppily handled, the interviews poorly conducted and critical evidence overlooked. Under the watchful eye of a newly-appointed Crime Investigations Manager, the team begin the painstaking process of tracing the original persons of interest.

Progress, however, is glacial, and so, when presented with proof that their progress is being monitored with alarming accuracy by someone who seems to always be one step ahead of the official investigation, Moran begins to wonder if he can make an arrest before the perpetrator falls into the hands of an antagonist with a very different idea of justice…

'Great story telling from a master of the crime thriller novel…'

In the Key of Death

The tranquility of a genteel household is shattered when an elderly piano teacher is found brutally murdered, leaving her sibling devastated and demanding answers. Enter DCI Brendan Moran, called out of retirement at short notice, to tackle the baffling case. As Moran delves deeper into the circumstances surrounding the murder, a web of complex connections and puzzling alibis among the suspects leave him struggling to pinpoint the elusive killer.

As the investigation intensifies, one of Moran's own team members becomes infatuated by the enigmatic leader of a self-sufficient commune, and suspicions are raised concerning a possible connection to the murder. With time running out, Moran must unravel the secrets concealed behind the commune's Utopian façade and navigate a dangerous labyrinth of deception to uncover the truth.

In the Key of Death intertwines themes of childhood trauma, psychological coercion and emotional manipulation – all wrapped up in a page-turning police procedural.

'...richly rewarding... Hunter spins a good tale...'

The Irish Detective 2 digital box set

The second omnibus edition of the popular DCI Brendan
Moran crime series by CWA shortlisted author, Scott Hunter.
Contents includes the fourth, fifth and sixth in series, plus an
exclusive short story 'Inside Job'...

**A Crime For All Seasons (short stories) - FREE via
website www.scott-hunter.net**

From the midwinter snowdrifts of an ancient Roman villa to a
summer stakeout at an exclusive art gallery, join DCI
Brendan Moran and his team for the first volume of
criminally cunning short stories in which the world-weary yet
engaging Irish detective reaffirms that there is indeed a crime
for all seasons...

'...great characters, plot lines and dialogue. More please!'

BookBub

has a New Release Alert.

Not only can you check out the latest deals, but you can also receive an email notifying you of my upcoming book publications by following me here:

https://www.bookbub.com/authors/scott-hunter

Website:

www.scott-hunter.net

Facebook:

https://www.facebook.com/scotttheword

Printed in Dunstable, United Kingdom

77206093R00143